Mattara

The Ventura Series

First Edition

C.A.Watts

Published in 2022 by
Ballads & Bards Bookhouse

Ballads & Bards Bookhouse
Wonnarua Country
AUSTRALIA
www.balladsandbardsbookhouse.com

A catalogue record of this work is available from the National Library of Australia

Mattara: The Ventura Series
ISBN: 978 0 6451408 8 0 (paperback)

10 9 8 7 6 5 4 3 2 1

Cover Design
Kozakura
Map Illustrator
Evin Kierans
Text Design
Istvan Szabo
Editor
Dr Danny Decillis

Printed by Ingram Spark, a Lightning Source company, and Kindle Direct Printing, an Amazon company.

Ballads & Bards Bookhouse acknowledges the Traditional Owners of the country on which we work, the Wonnarua and Awabakal nations, and recognises their continuing connection to their land, waters and culture. We pay respects to their Elders past, present and emerging.

Dedicated to my children,
For you I have worked so hard,
With you I love every moment of my life,
Because of you I am complete and whole.

Table of Contents

Prologue

The people of Valeria were rejoicing. The regime change from that of a matriarchal monarchy to an advisory board of equals had seen the quality of life rise astronomically all over the world. The long neglected fairies, sprites and pixies were finally feeling like they were on equal ground with the elves due to the shift in the balance of power.

Likewise, the elves, who had long had it ingrained in them that they had no value if they weren't in positions of power, felt a reprieve from such a burden. Many who had parents pushing them into political or other high achieving arenas, had cast of the weight of expectation aside, and were exploring obscure academia, arcane magic, the arts, and even community work due to their love of their homes and the people in it.

So much, did the people of Valeria love their new way of life that they had decided to re-elect Queen Eleria as their leader. While she watched fondly over her growing baby

Elora as she played by her desk, stacking blocks as high as she could reach, Queen Eleria continued reading through her first ever batch of monthly reports from her elven city officials.

She would meet with Evanna of the fairies, Glenrock of the sprites and Naevia of the pixies in the coming days to discuss any issues that had arisen in the time since Rogue and Ranger had left Valeria for the strange human world of their creator, accompanied by their beloved Guardian, Elva, who carried the Valerian Heart of Truth.

Much had changed since they had disappeared through one of the Queen's bathroom mirrors up on the third floor of the Marble Palace. Mostly for the better, such as her son's, Prince Fallon, marriage to Elva's brother, Fillipe. However, despite all the new wonderful things happening across the realm, the Queen was not aware that all over Valeria, a darkness was settling…

♠

The city of Port Nixin, once predominantly a city for pixies, the most diminutive of races, had expanded at a rapid rate. As such, it had become a hub for new business; taverns, jewellers, merchants, herbalists, potion makers, charm sellers of all types, had flocked to the city, as the lake provided an excellent import and export location for all of Valeria.

In one such tavern, a jovial crew had just recently arrived from having shipped a load of medical cargo from the Capitol, via Eliad. Elated from a successful voyage, round after round of drinks were consumed, until the entire crew had become red in the face. So merry did they become, in fact, that they didn't notice the cloaked stranger in the corner rise from a chair and exit the tavern, headed for their ship.

♠

On the other side of Valeria, in a building the size of a city itself, Ford, the Elven Advisor to the Observatory, and Elva's father, had been woken by a guard.

"What is it, Farrow?" he sternly asked the purple fairy guard who manned the main Observatory door. "It had better be a good one, your reason for waking me at this hour the night before my wife is due to return to the Capitol."

"I am sorry, Ford," the fairy said fearfully. "I knew you would not open the door for anyone but me and I would never bother you if it was not vitally important!"

"Then get on with it!"

"The medics, Sir," Farrow squeaked. "They found me on duty. It appe… well, it appears that Ariannah…"

"OUT WITH IT!"

"Sir, she seems to be waking!"

Ford immediately grabbed his travelling cloak and leapt

over the top railing of the Observatory, dropping the thirty levels to the main floor before rolling into a crouch and getting back to his feet, heading for the barred doors that led to the dungeons.

♠

Prince Fallon and Fillipe were on their honeymoon, gazing up the moons as they lay on the banks of Lake Viridian. They had only been married three days, but already they had planned their entire lives together.

After having spent much of his life assuming he would be forced into a marriage his father deemed appropriate, Prince Fallon had never even thought about the life he had the potential to lead with his true love. Now that his dream had come true, they had discussed everything from pets, to children, to their duties as active royals.

As they were not on the panel of advisors, they had no actual authority, but as members of the royal family it remained a standard expectation to serve Valeria. Both of the young men had agreed early on what exactly their focus would be: children; their safety and education. Step one was already in the works, with every orphanage in Valeria being turned into a boarding school and filled with the best teachers, healers, chefs and masters Valeria had to offer.

It had been found that a significant portion of the children in Valeria's orphanages were halfling children; that is, they were a mix of elf, fairy, sprite and pixie. As Fallon and Fillipe lay by the water, they spoke animatedly about how, by ensuring the growing generations were highly educated and well cared for, they could eradicate the stigma surrounding cross breeding forever.

♠

Back at the Observatory, Ariannah was stirring in her sleep. Her forehead was slick with sweat and her breath was coming in short gasps. As she lay in the crystal case, under the watch of guards and healers that monitored her around the clock, she dreamed…

A man is walking briskly along a long, stone hallway, his shoes rapping on the floor as he walks. His heart is racing as he follows the familiar route; down a narrow staircase and through an archway that leads into a large chamber.

There are no windows in the room, only a large pedestal standing on a raised platform in the centre of the space. Instead of paintings or tapestries hanging from the walls, there are seven giant mirrors; three on each side wall and one hanging opposite the door. Between each of the mirrors is a series of runes written in an ancient language.

The man is desperate. The mirror directly to his left is sparkling, like it is full of glitter. To his right, a second mirror has begun glowing a bright blue. As he steps closer, the mirror begins to ripple, like waves on the ocean...

CHAPTER 1

Culture Shock

§§

We were standing on the third floor foyer of Ventura Castle. Elva's eyes were wide as she gazed out of the window, looking towards the forest in the distance. She was speechless.

"Do you like it?" I asked, smiling.

"It's incredible," she breathed. "I've never seen anything like it!"

Elva had only just joined my sister Rogue and me in our world. For the past several weeks we had been in Elva's; Valeria, the Plains world of the Fae. It was a far more naturalistic world than ours, and felt all the more magical for it.

"It's no Marble Palace, but it's home," Rogue said.

"She said from the third floor of a castle," I snorted derisively.

Elva turned back to us, her eyes shining. I was still struggling to take her in. Her legs were covered in three-quarter denim shorts and her shoes were flat, leather boots. She wore a plain black tank top and her eyes had returned to their normal, icy blue. Her fairy wings had disappeared, as had the sharpness in her elven ears and the almond shape of her eyes. She was human.

"Uncanny," I breathed, shaking my head as I examined her face.

"What is it?" she said, touching her face. When she reached her ears, she froze, feeling the unfamiliar curve. "Oh! I'm-?"

"-Yep," Rogue said.

"I'm not-?"

"-Nope."

She seemed to have an internal argument with herself, before taking a deep breath to calm herself down. "What do we do now?"

"Search the bathrooms," Rogue sighed. "Starting on the fifth floor."

We had... er... *collected* Elva, as it were, from her world for a very specific reason. My name is Ranger, and a few months prior, my twin sister Rogue and me had inherited Ventura Castle and its surrounding estate from my Grandma Reina.

When we got here, we learned that it was in danger. Our ancestor Romira Royce had built the estate, and with it, seven mirrors. These mirrors lead to the different Venturan worlds, the first in which we found Elva, the Guardian of Valeria. Her job was to protect the Heart of Valeria and use the Heart to protect its world.

The problem was… we needed it. Romira's son Raphael, even as an ancient spirit, wanted Ventura and its worlds for his own, so to protect the worlds forever more, Romira had sacrificed himself to give his heart to the estate.

When it appeared Raphael was going to take the Heart of Ventura, his wife Raven stole it. She travelled to each of the Venturan worlds and gave them each a piece to protect themselves against Raphael… the Valerian piece Elva now wore around her neck in a silver locket.

So they were a package deal. We needed the Heart but Heart needed its Guardian, and so here Elva was, in our world, gazing at the majesty that was Ventura Castle and its grounds while we tried to find the location of the second mirror, which we believed to be in one of the bathrooms based on the clues we had been given. "No," I disagreed. "Not the bathrooms. Not yet." Rogue looked confused. "Almost a thousand years had passed in Valeria since Raven had left the Heart there," I reminded her.

Rogue's face dropped. "Mum and Dad," she whispered fearfully.

"We have to make sure they're ok before we leave again," I told them. "We can't leave not knowing."

"Well, the phones working would definitely be a good

sign," Rogue considered. "Sixth floor kitchen?"

"What's a *phone*?" Elva asked as I nodded.

"We'll show you," Rogue answered, heading for the staircase. Steadily, the feeling of dread and unease grew within us as we climbed towards the sixth floor.

"What is this?" Elva shivered violently as we reached the fourth floor landing. "This isn't what living in your world feels like, does it?"

"No… This is something else…" Rogue said, before looking at me. "We don't have a lot of time," she urged.

"Raphael?" I questioned. She nodded.

"Raphael?" Elva said quickly. "I know I said I could handle him if he came, but that was mostly for my parents' benefit. I have no idea how my magic, if I even have any, will work here! Just how much danger are we in?"

"His spirit still resides here, and it's definitely strong based on our last meeting." I said. "And we're vulnerable now because we've brought a part of the Heart of Ventura back here and we're in his territory."

Elva looked scared. "One piece of the Heart is not enough to defeat him,' Rogue went on. "But it *should* be enough to make him think twice about it. The higher danger will come later. Every time we come back with a Heart, he'll try to take the ones we have, and he'll be stronger every time."

"And if he succeeds?"

Neither of us answered.

We reached the sixth floor, which opened onto the grand dining room; a gigantic, glossy chandelier hanging from the ceiling above the twenty seater table. It felt like gravity had steadily been increasing on us. The air felt heavy and it was getting harder to breathe. "Are we close?" Elva puffed.

"The kitchen is through there," Rogue said breathlessly, pointing to the door on the left. The phone was on the other side, attached to the wall. She picked it up and held it to her ear. "Dial tone," she said quietly. "That's something at least." Elva watched Rogue work the strange machine curiously.

The phone rang twice before the hotel answered. "Hi, I need to confirm our last stay dates?" she asked politely. "Richard and Lyla Royce?" There was a pause. "Oh?" Her face showed utter confusion. "Ok... thank you." She hung up the phone and turned to us. "Mum and Dad are still there," she told us. "They only checked in a *week* ago."

"How is that possible?" I asked, gobsmacked.

"Why, what's wrong?" Elva questioned, still eyeing off the phone. "Your parents are safe. That's good, right?"

"Yes, it is," I confirmed, nodding. "But when we were in Valeria, we found out that time moved differently." Elva looked confused.

"While 300 years had passed since Romira built Ventura here, over *900* years had passed there," Rogue continued. "I don't know what we expected when we came back, but I don't think either of us expected this..."

"There's been a time shift… and now Valeria is moving at the same pace as here," I finished. Elva's confusion turned to shock.

"It's a relief, but definitely odd," Rogue said. "I thought we would've lost at least three weeks based on the time difference."

"I'm more worried about where we go next," I replied. "We have no idea how it will impact the passage of time."

"We didn't for Valeria either," Rogue pointed out.

"That was before we knew that possibility existed!" I exclaimed.

Elva had become increasingly agitated throughout the exchange. "Stop!" she suddenly yelled. "Don't you get it?" We stared back at her dumbly. I shrugged. "It's you!"

"What's us?" Rogue asked.

"The time change! You went to Valeria and the timelines in both worlds began running parallel," she explained. "It doesn't explain *why*, but it's the only logical explanation as to *what* happened."

"How do we know it wasn't you coming *back* with us that caused it?" I countered.

"I came back with you less than an hour ago. The timeline clearly synced long before that, or a lot more time would have pass~" Elva's reasoning was cut short with the slamming of a door. "What was that?"

We paused, looking around slowly. "Raphael," I said

softly.

"He can *move* things?" Elva gasped. "But he's supposed to be *dead?*"

"So is Romira, but you've literally got him around your neck like a dog in a designer handbag!" I retorted.

"*What does that even mean?*" she squeaked, hands ravelling through her necklace cord that held the Heart of Valeria, a piece that would eventually join the others to become the Heart of Ventura once more.

"Why do you think we're trying so hard to reunite the Heart?" Rogue cut us off, exiting the kitchen. "It's the only thing strong enough to get rid of him for good. Moving things is just one thing he keeps in his bags of tricks. Let's get this search going."

"Starting with the fifth floor," I reminded her as we headed back to the stairs. "It's clearly the front runner based on our research."

"Because of the bath?" Elva asked.

"You'll see," Rogue answered. "The phrase 'fit for a Queen' will make sense, you can count on that." What we didn't count on was a cold draught blowing through the foyer the moment we hit the stairs, chilling us all to the bone.

"Time to get moving," I whispered, struggling to breathe. We sprinted down the stairs as fast as our human feet could carry us. I missed my wings more than I cared to admit.

The moment we hit the fifth floor, a low moan began from

below us, rattling the stone under our feet. "GO!" Rogue screamed. "ON THE LEFT!" We each skidded to a stop near the end of the hallway and threw ourselves through the ornate door, one by one. Once inside, Rogue slammed the door and bolted it shut.

"What do you think *that* will do?" I yelled at her, throwing up my arms.

"I DON'T SEE *YOU* HELPING!"

"This is a bath?" Elva's voice cut in, panting heavily. "I've never seen one like it in all my life." The bathroom was floor to ceiling tile, in the palest blue. In the centre, on a large platform, sat the bath; a three by three metre square with delicately designed brass taps.

"It's a spa," Rogue said quickly. "It has jets and makes fancy bubbles that massage you and stuff. People use them to relax."

A low banging started coming from the door Rogue had bolted shut. "Occupied!" I called out.

"Ranger!" Elva hissed. "*I didn't come here so you could get me killed!*"

"If he gets in, the reason you came here will be pretty irrelevant for all of us," I pointed out, as we jumped up the stairs and onto the platform.

The three of us stared into the depths of the water, but after a few moments, my eyes drifted to the white substance that made up the spa's edges. I noticed the intricate detail of the carved surface I'd never noticed before. There were fish swimming among seaweed, and at the corner, opposite the taps, was one word. "Mattara," I said in a hushed whisper, running my fingers over the carved word. "I've got it!"

Just as Elva and Rogue came to examine the carving, the door to the bathroom was blown off its hinges.

'GET IN!" I screamed, throwing Elva into the spa. She arched over and fell in, screaming as she disappeared from sight completely.

"She's gone!"

"Yep."

"Ready?" Rogue asked. I nodded. She grabbed a hold of me and together, we threw ourselves into the water.

CHAPTER 2
Fish Out of Water…
Metaphorically Speaking

§§

For just a moment, we were suspended in a bright white nothingness, then we were falling. It wasn't like when we fell into Valeria; this was much more pressurised, as though we weren't actually falling, but being pushed through soft jelly at lightning speed. It was the strangest sensation. When we finally began to slow down, I realised that it wasn't a strange substance at all. It was water.

I immediately began panicking. I started to scream as I hit the ocean floor… then realised I could breathe. My heart still racing, I immediately looked around for Rogue and Elva. They were a few feet away from me, lying on the soft sand of the ocean floor.

"Are you ok?" I called to them, closing my eyes and massaging my temples.

"We're breathing… underwater!" I heard Elva cry out in astonishment as she sat up.

"Ranger!" Rogue gasped.

"What is it?" I asked, opening my eyes. There she was, well, half of her at least. Her top half was human, covered by large, overlapping, blue seashells. Her hair was electric blue, and her eyes were dark, much darker than they'd been before. Her bottom half was the most surprising, for it was the same colour as her hair, and in the form of a long, scaly tail.

Here we go again… I sighed internally.

A mermaid. Several bubbles floated out of my mouth.

"What are you?" Elva yelped as she looked up at Rogue, then down at herself. "WHAT IS THAT?" Elva was purple. Her hair had grown past her waist in fuchsia ringlets and her eyes were violet. She seemed to be wearing a pink halter top, and her tail was deep purple, ending in one large circular fin patterned with delicate lavender filigree.

"We're mermaids," Rogue answered her, pointing. "That's a tail." I got a glimpse of bottle green as I looked down and my head snapped back up in shock. Mermaids… of course. We'd changed when we arrived in Valeria, logically they same would occur for the other worlds too.

"Who are you?" a soft voice asked. It belonged to a small mergirl. She had short, blonde hair with a small pink starfish on one side. Her tail was a bright yellow and ended in two small fins. "No one is 'posed to *be* here," she said.

"My name is Ranger," I told her, and watched as her eyes widened.

Before she could say anything else, a high, shrill voice called out. "Lani!" We turned and found that we were in the front yard of a cottage made of stacked stones and surrounded by enormous corals of all colours. A woman had slammed open the large shell door and was running, well, swimming, towards her daughter. She pulled her up into her arms and held her close.

The woman had long locks of strawberry blonde hair that hung over her shoulders and she wore a white tank top. Her tail was pale orange and she had four oval, scalloped fins, patterned in yellow. "Who are you?" she hissed suspiciously.

"She said her name is Ranger, Mummy!" the child named Lani said excitedly, eyes wide. She clearly didn't come across a lot of new people. She stared at Rogue's ruffled fin in fascination.

"What?" she gasped, looking back to us and frowning slightly, tightening her grip on her daughter.

"My name is Ranger. This is my sister, Rogue, and our friend, Elva."

"Rogue and Ranger," she scoffed. "What a joke."

"And what do you mean by that?" Rogue said irritably, her tail thrashing in her anger.

"Rogue and Ranger? The figures of legend? You *really* expect me to believe that?"

"It's no business of ours if you do," I told her calmly, looking around. There seemed be nothing else around us as far as I could see. "Where are we?"

"You're in the Centre, as you very well know!" the woman began to rant. "Countless tourists coming here despite the danger, trying to make a name for themselves! The Guardian should be ashamed of herself, calling for the public to do her job! People are getting hurt while she just watches!"

"Guardian?" I questioned. "The Guardian is sending people here? Why?"

"They came from the High Place, Mummy!" Lani cried out again before the woman could respond.

"The High Place?" her mother repeated, shocked. "You came from above? How is that possible?"

"We told you how. You didn't believe us," I replied.

"In case you haven't noticed, we're not from around here," Elva put in defensively.

The woman's face had changed. She was now looking highly distressed. "Come inside. Quickly!" she hissed, hurrying through the shell door. The inside of the cottage was light and airy. Kelp curtains covered the windows and a large, round boulder acted as the kitchen table. Off to the left, an open clam shell bed could be seen through a doorway.

Once we'd followed her inside, she closed the door and bolted it shut. "What were you thinking, coming here?" she started, directing us to the living room area. There were several brightly coloured anemones along the wall, and large yellow sea sponge opposite them acting as a lounge chair.

"What do you mean?" I asked, sitting down, as Lani was placed at the large boulder table with some books.

"You came through the mirror? You found the carvings on the bath?" she started again, gaining momentum.

"How do you kn~" Rogue began, leaping up and looking startled.

"*~It doesn't matter how I know!*" she yelled back, waving her hands around emphatically. "The only thing that matters is getting you out of here, *now!*"

"We're not going anywhere until you start explaining yourself!" I snapped. "Who are you? How do you know us? And why is it so important for us to leave?" I demanded to know. This woman knew something. We weren't going to leave until she gave it up.

"Oh, don't give me that look!" she growled. "I invented that!"

"What is *that* supposed to mean?" Rogue burst out. Elva just sat there, watching the verbal ping~pong. It was obvious she had no idea what was going on; not that I knew any better.

The woman looked anxious, but she took a deep breath and tried to force herself to calm down. "My name is Anomar," she said, sitting down. "This is my daughter, Lani."

"And?" Rogue questioned, urging her on.

"I know you and your family. I've known them all my

life," she continued. "This is called the Centre. Three cities of Mattara; Medina, Coral Ridge, and Caelios; are linked by three roads; Lord's Way, Manta Tide, and the Marina, or Guardian Crossing."

"Why is the road called that?" Elva asked quickly.

"The name of that road changes with every new Guardian. The current Guardian's name is Marina," she explained. "I take it that you know what a Guardian is and what exactly it is they're guarding?" I raised my eyebrow but didn't respond. Even *I* knew better than that. "Yes, of course you do; why else would you be here?" she said exasperatedly. "The Centre is the area inside the triangle made by the cities and their linking roads."

"And we shouldn't be here because…?" Rogue pressed, nodding her head for Anomar to go on.

"The Centre has been facing dangers of late. Multiple cities and towns becoming the target of horrendous attacks; explosions, kidnappings, deaths; the people are terrified," she told us. "After certain investigations, the Centre was found to be the home or sanctuary of the creature responsible… the hiding place of the Destroyer.

"What's… the Destroyer?" Elva asked softly, frowning.

"Nobody knows who or what it is. All we know is that it wreaks havoc and destruction wherever it can. Everything goes black and suddenly a building is in ruins or a whole house of people have disappeared." She sighed, sadness on her face. "No one who has been taken has been seen since. The Guardian has announced that anyone who can stop the Destroyer or provide information leading to its capture will be rewarded. It's caused all manner of people coming here trying to find it, hoping it will lead to them getting riches and fame; or even more stupidly, the Guardian's hand."

"When did this start?" I asked.

"The announcement was made a little less than a month ago, maybe?" she answered. "The Destroyer has always existed, but it only ever attacked those who came across it unknowingly, and only ever here in the Centre; its territory. About three weeks ago something changed," she went on. "It started seeking out targets, wiping out whole villages at once."

"That was when Grandma died" Rogue said to me.

"What?" Anomar gasped. "Yo- your grandma died?"

"Yeah; almost a month ago," I answered. "Why?"

"So *that's* why this is happening!" she cried. "This is because of *you!*"

"What's because of us?"

"Isn't it obvious?" she said, pulling at her fingertips. "It was created and put here to wait for you! To stop you from getting to the Guardian and the Heart of Mattara! This is about Ventura!"

"How do *you* know about Ventura?" Elva asked, getting up. "No one in my world had ever heard of it except the

Guardians before Rogue and Ranger came!"

"Your world?" she looked stunned, her mouth agape. "There are others?"

I studied Anomar's face. One thing had been clear from the moment she'd mentioned the mirror; she wasn't from Mattara any more than we were, but I'd realised something else. Looking at her and the way she flicked her nails; the way she'd said: '*I invented that*' was all too familiar. It finally hit me how she knew us and what we were doing. The realisation almost knocked me off my chair. "Anomar."

"What?"

"Your name," I said. "You never did have any imagination… did you Ramona?"

CHAPTER 3
Family Reunion

§§

"What?" she hissed. "How did you-?"

"-Spelling your name backwards won't get you far," I sighed.

Rogue's eyes had widened. She was shaking her head in astonishment. "Ramona?" she whispered. "Is it really you?"

Ramona; the daughter of our long lost Aunty Rhiannon. After Rhiannon had disappeared more than ten years ago, Ramona had been adamant that something had 'taken' her. Angry that no one would listen, she cut off the family and hadn't been heard from since.

Ramona appeared to collapse in on herself. Had we not been underwater, I felt like she would have started crying. "Yes… it's me."

"Have you been here the whole time?" I asked her. "You disappeared over a decade ago!"

"A decade?" she sat back down on her sea sponge sofa. "It's only been five years here," her voice dropped off. "And

I've been here the whole time, since three days after Mum disappeared. No wonder you've grown so much I didn't recognise you."

"What's going on?" Elva suddenly interrupted. "Who is she?" In all the confusion, we'd forgotten she was even there.

"Elva, Ramona, or Anomar, is our cousin; from our world. Her mother, our Aunty Rhiannon, disappeared years ago. Ramona left not long after, when she was seventeen, and hasn't been seen since," I explained to her.

"Why did you come here?" Elva asked Ramona curiously. "How did you even *get* here? I mean, how did you learn about the mirrors?"

Ramona took a deep breath and closed her eyes. "The last time I was in the castle, when we were all there for Mum's funeral, I got into an argument with Uncle Reiner," she began. "No one was *listening* to me when I was telling them what I saw! They thought I was dreaming, or hallucinating from the trauma." She scoffed.

"What do you mean?" Elva asked quietly, enraptured.

"Mum didn't take off. She didn't run away; she was *taken*," Ramona said. "I was there. Grand-" her voice caught in her throat. "Grandma had just gotten over the flu and Mum and me had been staying with her until she got better.

"We lost heat," she continued, her eyes gazing across the room. "Rather than call for someone, Mum went down to the furnace to see what was happening. After she'd gone down there I started hearing weird noises. I just thought it was Mum playing with the levers and valves down there, so I ignored it, but when I heard her yell, I went to the doorway to check it out.

"I'd always been scared of the furnace, so I avoided it wherever I could," she slammed her hands on her lap. "I hesitated! I was too scared to go down and I FROZE!" Despite being unable to cry, Ramona started to sob.

Lani climbed down from the table and swam over to her mother. She let herself drop into her mother's lap and hugged her tightly. "It's ok Mummy," she said, patting her head. "It'll be alright." Ramona held her daughter tightly, while her body shook.

"I love you," she whispered to Lani, before looking back up at us. "By the time I got down there, Mum was gone. I looked all around the room, thinking maybe she'd fallen and hurt herself... but she had completely vanished. Then... I heard *laughing*."

"Laughing?" I repeated.

"It was like it was coming from the walls," she said softly, fear in her eyes from the memory.

"And your family didn't believe you?" Elva asked. "What do they believe happened to her?"

"They think she took off with a bunch of Grandma's money and never looked back."

"Wait, then what was the point of the funeral?" I was

getting more confused with every skeleton coming out of the family closet.

At this, Ramona's eyes flashed angrily. "Reiner insisted," she spat poisonously. "Despite believing she was alive, he had a life insurance policy that wouldn't pay out without a death certificate, which a judge would only release if there was a funeral."

"WOW!" Rogue said loudly. "That man has no boundaries, does he?"

"But that doesn't explain how you ended up here?" Elva pointed out.

"No," Ramona agreed, rubbing her eyes. "After I found out about the life insurance policy, I confronted Reiner. He insisted it had to be done because *he* would be the one 'footing the bill' for me," she said, disgust on her face. "I told him that if he even tried to claim it, I'd report him for fraud. He was so mad… After the argument, I didn't want to deal with him or anyone else, so I went upstairs. I was in the spa on the-"

"-Fifth floor," Rogue cut her off.

"Yes," she nodded. "I was pushed under the water. Just when I thought I was going to die, I found that I could breathe, and here I was."

"Do you have any idea who did it?" I asked her. "Were you looking for the Mattara mirror?"

"I didn't even *know* about it until I got here!" she exclaimed. "Since I've come here I learned all about Romira and how Mattara came to exist; the story of Raven coming and granting the world a piece of his Heart," she paused. "The only thing I can think of about why someone would want me dead is…"

"What?" Elva asked hurriedly.

"Was that it was Raphael, and he thought I was one of you," she said. "The family that used to live here took me in. I had Lani three years ago. They're in Caelios now. It was too dangerous for them to stay."

"Why did you stay here?" I asked her.

"This is the Entrance. If you come through the mirror, you end up here. I knew that when the time came and you found your way here, this is where you'd be," she explained. "The Destroyer has got to be here because this is where it would have ended up when Raphael sent it. He must have realised that I'd gone through to another world when he tried to kill me!"

"And that's how he knew where we were going!" Elva exclaimed, holding her hand over her mouth. "He knew where we'd find the mirror! Which also means that~"

"~That he already would have alerted the Destroyer to our presence already," Rogue finished for her.

"I'm afraid so," Ramona sighed solemnly. "The Destroyer has caused nothing but grief and pain. It is a being of pure chaos and it doesn't differentiate. It will target *anybody*.

"That's why you've been chasing off anyone in the

Centre," Elva concluded. "To protect them."

"As much as I can, at least. Fame seekers are a moronic bunch."

"Which is why we need to leave right now," Rogue announced, getting out of her chair and heading for the door.

"No," Ramona cut her off. "It's late. You'll leave in the morning."

"With us here, both you and your daughter are prime targets," I pointed out, heading for the door. "We can't do that to you."

Ramona didn't look comfortable with the idea of us leaving, but it was obvious we weren't going to accept the risk to her family. She slid open the bolt and looked outside. "It's clear, for now. You need to be fast. Every second you're here is a second the Destroyer knows *exactly* where to find you," she whispered.

"Where do we find the Guardian?" I asked her.

"Go to the main city of Medina, to the north. In two days, you'll reach a small village. It's called the Protected Village, because the Destroyer cannot get inside. There, you can get an escort to the city that will protect you from the Destroyer. They've started banding together and forming security details," she rolled her eyes. "They're idiots if they think any number of them can stand against the Destroyer, but it's better than having it find you alone. You'll find what you need at Medina when you arrive."

She ushered us outside and suddenly became very serious. "Girls… I beg you not to reveal who I am to this world. I've created a life for myself here and I don't want to lose it. Will you keep what you've learned to yourselves?"

There was a silence that pressed down on us like the many thousands of tons of water above, before Rogue swam forward. "We're sorry no one looked for you, or your mum. We're happy you were able to build a life for yourself after you lost her. We promise we won't tell a soul," she said.

"Thank you," Ramona whispered, holding her daughter tightly.

We turned away and hadn't gone ten feet, when we heard Lani's small voice call out: "You're going to come back, right?"

She stared at us, her eyes wide and her mouth slightly open. We laughed. "We promise!" we called back.

♠

We were glad the trip to the village only took two days, because the second we left the sight of the small house on the sandy plain of the Centre, a cold feeling stole into us. By the end of the first day, we were practically shivering with cold dread.

"This is horrible. Someone distract me," I asked, wheezing slightly.

"Elva, tell us about Valeria," Rogue said. "We never did get to learn much while we were there."

"Well," Elva huffed. "First off, the lot of us are freaks of nature."

"Oh? What do you mean?"

"Well you, me and Ranger could tap into the magic of the plains really easily; I presume due to our connection to Romira, but that sort of magical efficacy is actually quite rare," she explained. "Most study their entire lives and never reach that level of mastery."

"Like at the Observatory?" I asked.

"Uh huh," she nodded. "All of creation within Valeria *is* innately magical, but to use it how we do is unheard of. There are only two seers in the entire Observatory that can call on their sight and actually receive an answer."

"What did you do?" I asked. "You know, before you were the Guardian?"

"I was a Druid," she answered, moving to wipe sweat from her forehead despite being underwater. "I grew things."

"Magically?"

"Sometimes. I had a warm touch that could accelerate growth rates," she said. "But it didn't work on all plants and it didn't work all the time."

"What plants wouldn't it work on?" Rogue asked curiously.

"The sentient ones," she said simply, grasping at a stitch

in her side. "It becomes an ethical dilemma during training when a family of roses snaps at you to 'bugger off'. You tend to avoid trying after that." Rogue and I fell silent at the thought.

That night, when we finally decided we had to stop or risk falling asleep as we swam, the heavy blackness invaded our dreams, turning light into shadows and colours into darkness that taunted us.

When we awoke the next morning, Elva was crying, clutching the necklace at her throat. "Heart of Valeria, help me! *I can't take this any longer!*"

"We don't have much of a choice," I said softly, holding her as she sobbed. "We're going to get you through this, Elva," I promised her. "It'll get easier once we reach the village, you'll see."

"What if I feel like this because I'm not meant to be here?"

"We all feel it, Elva," Rogue told her, rolling her neck in her hand. "It's like… the water is heavy? Like the sand is trying to swallow me."

"It's the Destroyer," I said. "When the time comes, we'll take it down just like we did Ariannah." Ariannah had almost destroyed Valeria in an attempt to take control of the crown. For some reason, the power of the Heart of Truth, Valeria's Heart, didn't affect her. Only with all three of us had we been able to overpower her, and even then, Elva could only put her into an enchanted sleep.

"But she was Valerian, and belonged there. This Destroyer is something else. What if our powers aren't enough here because it's not our world?" Elva rambled worriedly.

"It's a good thing that we won't be alone then, huh" Rogue replied. "We needed you in Valeria and we need the Guardian of Mattara here. If we can't do it alone, we can do it with their help."

"That's right," I agreed. "It's why they exist. It's what they're made for. We just have to find them."

Elva hiccupped and shakily got up. "That's why we exist," she repeated to herself.

We refused to stop until we reached the village after that. We knew that if we paused for even a moment, we'd lose the will to continue and Ventura would be lost. It meant that we pushed on throughout the night, sometimes almost crawling along the sandy ocean floor that was steadily turning rocky.

By the time the village was in sight, the night ocean darkness was starting to lighten as dawn approached. We were stumbling over our own tails, near exhaustion, when we finally crossed the border.

"Oh my!" a voice cried out. In moments, three sets of strong hands were lifting us out of the sand and carrying us away.

CHAPTER 4

Armoured Guard

§§

When I awoke, I noticed something was covering my eyes. I removed it; the soft, yellow sea sponge; and found myself in a large white room, surrounded by bright lights. As my eyes focused, I saw that the lights were glow worms that had been placed in white coral and set into the walls. I tried to sit up, but my body was heavy and slow. I cried out and fell back onto the soft mattress, before hearing movement by my side.

"Hello Miss, how are you feeling?" a deep voice asked.

I turned my head and almost choked. From the waist up was a perfectly normal man, but instead of a tail finishing him, his bottom half was eight black tentacles, the undersides a deep, royal blue. "Octopus!" I squeaked.

"What was that, sorry?" he asked, turning to me. His skin was pale green, but his eyes and hair were dark brown, his hair in one long plait. He was smiling, but the figure still looked strangely eerie.

40

"Nothing," I blushed. "Where am I?"

"You're in a medical tent. The dark magic affected you and your companions quite badly," he answered, looking at a clipboard on the end of the bed. "They're already awake and answering a few questions. I was sent to see how you are."

"Ok?" I breathed, still stunned by his visage.

"Can you explain to me why you collapsed at our village border?" he asked.

"I have no idea. We were travelling from a relative's home," I lied, before remembering what Ramona had told us about the Centre. "In Caelios."

"So you have no idea why you lost consciousness?" he pressed.

"I guess we must have pushed ourselves too hard."

"Well, I can assure you, your exhaustion has nothing to do with your travels. All three of you were shivering and rambling nonsense," he went on, coral pen to his clipboard. "From my experience, I would say you've spent too much time in the Destroyer's territory."

My breath caught in my chest. What had we said? Had we given ourselves away? If he knew we'd been in the Centre would we be in trouble? The panic must have shown on my face. "Do not fear," he reassured me, placing his hand on my shoulder. "It happens to many people. The longer you're in its territory, the more it wants you gone."

I began to breathe easier. So, the Destroyer didn't just look for us, but all people in its territory. "The feeling should dissipate soon," the Octopus man's voice cut through my thoughts. "We have expert witches that protect our village from the Destroyer's effects. They are highly skilled. They're the only reason our community has continued to thrive here!

"By the look of how quickly you've deteriorated, the Destroyer has chosen you. Don't worry!" he laughed at the look on my face. "Once you've restored yourselves, we'll have you escorted to Medina and I expect the next time you travel, you'll use the roads provided now, wont you?"

"Oh, of course!" I said, smiling and nodding. "Where are the others? My friends?" I asked him.

"They're out in the courtyard. Being outside with the light and colour does wonders for those affected by the Destroyer. We believe it is due to the draining, depressive effect it has on its victims," he answered, looking up from the clipboard. "You can go see them if you wish. The door is just through there." He pointed to the large open doorway at the back of the room.

I got out of bed and in an attempt to swim, got tangled in the bars of the end of the bed. It was only then that I realised I didn't have a tail anymore. "Still a bit tight in the tentacles, are we?" The Octopus man helped me to my feet.

Smiling in embarrassment, I swam out the back door as best I could in my new form. Seeing that the whole village was made of Octopus people, I understood why Elva and

Rogue had also sprouted tentacles. They were sitting in a quiet corner of the village square in a desperate struggle to untangle themselves from each other.

Laughing to myself, I swam over. They were yelling at each other. "Put it through there!" Elva was whining. "You're only tangling it more!"

"I am not!" Rogue snapped, pulling on one of the tangled tentacles. "This is the way it has to go-!"

"-Ouch! That's mine!"

"Hey, you're awake!" Rogue exclaimed, finally noticing me as I stood there with my arms crossed, watching the exchange.

"Are you feeling ok?" Elva asked anxiously.

"I'll be fine," I sighed. "Let me help." They both folded their arms and slowly but surely, I weaved my way through all sixteen tentacles, eventually freeing them both.

"Oh, that's better!" Elva breathed happily. "Why are we like this? We were *mermaids* before."

"We change to blend in," I reminded her. "Just like Rogue and I did when we were in Valeria. We would be elves, or fairies, or sprites, based on who we were around. We could control it if we tried hard enough, but the body tends to default to the population around us if we don't pay attention. This village is nothing but Octopus people, so we changed to be one of them," I explained.

"What other types of people do you think we'll find

here?" Rogue asked, looking around expectantly.

"I saw a man with a shark tail before," Elva put in. "They are called triakis, and the octopus people? Those are cecaelia."

Rogue and I stopped, confused. "How do you~?"

"~Romira," she whispered, tapping her Guardian necklace. It flashed dully.

"You still have his memories? *Here?*"

"Not like back home… but I've been getting flashes; some dreams. I know enough to get us by."

We stopped talking as a thin woman approached us. Her eyes were grey and her eyebrows and eyelashes were pale. Her hair was all different shades of grey, but she didn't look at all old. Her lips were red and her skin was deep purple. We saw that her teeth were white and straight when she smiled at us. "Hello ladies," she said warmly.

"Hello," Elva replied. "Can we help you?"

"My name is Njeri," she introduced herself with a bow. "I am one of the mother witches here in Inkan Village. You were informed by the medic that the Destroyer has chosen you, correct?" she asked.

"What does *that* mean?" Elva asked.

"Yes," I nodded, concerned. "Why? What's happened?"

"Nothing at all, my dears. I am in charge of the security details. I'm here to tell you that an escort has been arranged for you for tomorrow morning," she informed us. "There are a few procedures that we need to go through. Will you follow me?"

"Oh! Thank you!" Rogue responded, getting up. We followed her through the village to the stables, where ten seahorses were in separate stalls.

"These four are Lightning, Storm, Bubbles and Needles," she began. "They are the four that will be taking you to Medina." She continued on quickly.

"We're taking seahorses?" I gaped. My distraction almost got me left behind, and I stumbled as I tried to catch back up.

We continued to follow her. She led us to a house in the square and let herself in. "Come, come girls!" At the end of the hallway was a door that led to an open sitting area. A group of people sat around a number of small tables.

They were all different races. A few were octopus… cecaelia? But others were merfolk, and I noticed one man with red eyes and a black shark tail. Elva had called them triakis. Others were none of these, but of a different race altogether that I was unable to recognise. They appeared to be made up of water and light particles. Some had legs and others had fins, but all seemed to be slightly transparent. The woman saw that we were staring and turned to us, still smiling warmly.

"It's all right. We won't hurt you."

Elva gave us a questioning look. "Naiads," I told her under my breath so they couldn't hear.

"Water spirits," Rogue elaborated.

"This is Maxima," Njeri introduced. "Mortima, Naira and Shoal. They will be your escorts."

"It's nice to meet you," Elva squeaked, her eyes stuck on Shoal the triakis. Her body shook slightly as he shook her hand.

Maxima and Mortima were mermaids, both red, and very clearly related. The naiad was called Naira, who nodded when we greeted them. Shoal the triakis was the biggest creature I'd ever seen. His shoulders were at least a metre wide and his chest was covered in the same dark, coarse hair that was on his head.

"A Naiad always travels with an escort, for the Destroyer cannot sense them, as they are a part of the water," Njeri told us. "Maxima will be driving the carriage and Mortima will ride inside with you. Shoal will ride alongside on a seahorse and Naira will be beside Maxima, acting as a scout. Any questions?"

I looked to Rogue and Elva for confirmation. We all shook our heads.

"Wonderful!" Njeri replied, clapping her hands together. "I will spend the next few hours weaving the protective spells around the carriage. By tomorrow morning, we'll be ready to send you on your way!"

"Thank you," I replied gratefully. We said goodbye to our escort and were taken to where we'd be spending the night.

Once alone, we thought over what our next step would be. Elva was still shivering. "These people are fish!" she squeaked in an attempt to express how overwhelmed she was feeling. "I… I used to go fishing with my father for octopus and barracuda! And now… now they're alive! And talking! And what if… what if-?"

"-What if the water species from Valeria had the same sentience and society and you never knew?" Rogue offered. Elva nodded, horror on her face.

"It's ok," I smiled, putting my arm around her. "It's all right. Rogue and me always used to go fishing. What we used to fish for is nothing compared to what these beings are. This world is full of real people living real lives. What you were able to fish out of Viridian Lake is completely different. You can't worry about it."

"But we don't know that!" she pressed. "Not for sure!" Elva went quiet, still looking rather disturbed by the world she was in. I felt like this was how people ended up choosing to be a vegetarian.

"Is something else wrong, Elva?" I asked her.

She was silent for a few moments before she answered. "It's my birthday in two days," she whispered. "I never expected to be away from my family. Birthdays were always a highly celebrated event in Valeria. Even when I was Guardian, I was able to go home for it. Between that and my brother's wedding… I'm missing so much." She laid back on the bed, covering her eyes with her hands.

"For a reason," I pointed out. "Valeria will be able to celebrate so many more birthdays because of what we're doing here."

"I just feel like I don't belong here," she said quietly.

"You would, because you don't," I said matter of factly. "You're a real fish out of water here!" I laughed at my own joke, before I turned to Rogue. She was looking at the Ventura blueprints and the mirror riddle. "How's it going?"

"Backwards," she frowned with a slight growl, putting down the blueprints. "I don't understand this one. '*The third where nature is lush and full of life, where they receive the most light. The pack will demand its due respect, for their triumphs and their might.*'"

"That could be anywhere," she groaned, waving her hands around. Her tentacles mimicked them comically. One got in the way and she accidentally whacked it. "*Ow!* The castle has plants in every room on every floor."

"Sounds like we're looking for the room with the most windows; on all the floors except the third and fifth. It talks about nature '*where they receive the most light*'," I said, pointing.

"Why won't they be on three or five?" Elva asked, lifting her head up once more, suddenly looking interested.

"The Valerian mirror was on third and the Mattaran mirror was on fifth," Rogue told her. "If there are seven mirrors and seven floors in the castle, it doesn't take a rocket scientist to figure out there's one on each floor."

"I suppose," she frowned, looking at the blueprints. "But that could be just what someone *wants* us to think."

"Well Raven hid the mirrors. She easily could have put in some sort of pattern to make it easier for us," Rogue said.

Elva didn't look convinced, but she dropped the subject. Rogue was never the one to take 'no' for an answer. Once she had something in her mind or she convinced herself she was right it would take several PhDs wheeling in trolleys full of peer reviewed articles to change her mind… and even then they'd probably find it harder than their dissertations.

Rogue was reserved and respectful for sure, and far more socially adept than I could *ever* be, but stubbornness was her fatal flaw. I could never figure out how she did it. She could debate with *anyone* and she would be spirited and passionate; I did it and I was disrespectful and argumentative. I tried to be like her, copy what she did, but people never reacted to me the way they did her. I guess it was her Rogue-ish charisma.

♠

We had just boarded the carriage by the northern entrance to the village. It was incredible; a half open giant clam in a rich yellow colour. A pale pink water weed formed the upper canopy and kept us out of sight.

Mortima was sitting with Rogue, across from Elva and me. We could hear Njeri and Shoal speaking just outside the door. Naira and Maxima had already taken up their positions in the driver seats at the front.

"Are you ready?" Mortima asked us.

"Ready for what?" Elva replied, her anxiety returning.

"If the Destroyer comes for you en route, you need to be prepared," he told us. "The moment Naira gives the word; you are to remain still and silent. They will soon get back to us with news of whether or not the danger has passed. If it turns out the Destroyer has sighted and locked on us, they will directly intercept it and Maxima will put the horses to their top speed."

"Why don't they go their fastest to begin with?" Elva asked. "Where I'm from, horses can run or walk and use the same amount of energy. Why not run the whole time?"

Mortima nodded understandingly. "Should a danger that is not the Destroyer see us speeding through the Centre as though the devil himself were pursuing us, the more curious it will become and the more chance there will be of it attacking us. We want to avoid that at all cost," he explained, looking out of the window. "Because then we run the risk of having multiple predators on our tails."

"How long will this take?" I asked, as the village fell out of sight and the all too familiar feeling of dread settled upon me.

"In this carriage and with these horses, we'll arrive in Medina tomorrow," he answered.

I began to breathe easier. Knowing that the strange, deathly feeling would not be drilling into our minds and hearts for as long as it had before, made the trip to Medina seem a lot more bearable.

Over the next day, I fell asleep twice; both times waking to the sound of Mortima's voice as he spoke to the driver, whom we had learned was his sister; Maxima. Four times, Naira had alerted us to danger in the waters. All four times we'd stayed still and silent as Mortima listened; and all four times, we sighed with relief as Naira conveyed the message that the danger had passed. It was not the Destroyer; not this time.

Curiously, every time we saw Naira, if we could actually see them at all in the water, they looked different. First they had hair longer than their body, covering their Greek style chiton, then it was in a bun on top of their head while they wore a saddle bag over one shoulder and had three separate mermaid tails, then it was short and cropped, exposing broad shoulders sticking out of a transparent tank top.

"Illusionists?" I whispered to Rogue. "Shapeshifters?"

"In a sense," Elva answered softly. "Being the very water itself they are ever changing."

We were interrupted by a sharp voice hissing through the wall of the carriage, like it was right beside us, so that our hearts clenched with horror.

"It is the Destroyer!" Naira whispered loudly. "Moving to intercept!" The voice sounded fainter and fainter as it whizzed away from the carriage. We all stayed still and silent, terror keeping us in our place. In the driver's seat, Maxima called to the seahorses, urging them on. A second later, we heard the crack of a whip and felt the carriage lurch forward as it readily gained speed. The seahorses knew what they had to do; they were ready.

We almost screamed as the door to the carriage flew open. Mortima leapt across the doorway in readiness, but it was only Shoal.

"What is happening?" Mortima asked him quietly.

"Naira has forced it into open combat," he replied in a soft voice, closing the door behind him. "It is occupied for the moment, but I fear Naira will lose. If it flees, they won't be able to pursue it fast enough."

"How could Naira lose?" Rogue asked Shoal, eyes wide with fear.

"The Destroyer fights as one that has nothing to lose and everything to gain. Naira has unrivalled skill, but has not fought the likes of the Destroyer in this manner," Shoal told her, his red eyes blazing. "We have never seen it battle so hard in order to gain its wanted victim; not like this. It is strange." He gazed out the window.

I shrugged and looked away, going slightly red. We all

knew very well why the Destroyer was trying to get us to us so badly. After waiting so long, it had finally found what it had been sent here for. It wasn't about to let us get away.

"Happy birthday to me… Happy birthday to me…" Elva sang softly.

CHAPTER 5
The High Council

§§

"Happy birthday to you… Happy birthday to you…" Far away, by any measure of distance, in the world of Valeria, Elva's mother sang back. Evanna was moving along the walkway that ran around the outside of the Marble Palace, in the Capitol of Levindra. She had a meeting with the Queen and the other Advisors to the Crown, but she was in no rush to attend.

Evanna was missing her family terribly. Her son, of whom she was so proud, had been in North-East Point for almost a week now, overseeing the reconstruction of the newly renamed Archer Conservatorium of Divination. As each orphanage had been rebuilt, revamped and rebranded, each had also been given a task; to evaluate and analyse each child in its care, and ensure they were placed correctly based on their skills and interests. By doing so, Valeria ensured that every child could maximise its potential.

In North-East Point, due to its proximity to the

Observatory, the Archer Conservatorium would cultivate the knowledge and skills of astronomers in training, in readiness for when they could apply to become an apprentice. There, they would join the ranks of the star gazers who spent their lives divining the future of Valeria from its constellations.

Evanna was incredibly proud of what her son and his husband, Prince Fallon, were accomplishing. The Arcana Institute of Magic in Eliad, the Alethea School of Healers in Farivian, the Flora and Fauna Nature House on the banks of the Veritann River, and String's Conservatory of the Arts in Faeorah had been completed in just a few short weeks.

Educators and house parents had been brought in care to for and evaluate the kids, while healers and therapists came to ensure their body was healthy and that they felt safe and secure. It was a lot of change for small children, and after being neglected under the traditional regime prior to the Advisory Council being developed, Prince Fallon and Fillipe, Evanna's son, were committed to getting it right.

Evanna's husband, Ford, had been locked away in the Observatory for weeks. She hadn't even been able to speak to him for longer than a minute at each of the four times she had actually been able to catch him at all. Something was happening, and while he would never lie to her, he wasn't forthcoming with information either.

Evanna strode through the main doors and headed for the meeting chamber, thinking of her daughter. Elva was 21 today. There would be no celebration. As far as Valeria was aware, the Guardian remained in her stronghold, guarding the Heart of Truth. It was too dangerous to announce the birthday of a Guardian at the best of times, for fear they would be targeted on their home visit; now, it was impossible. If too much attention was drawn to Elva, someone was more likely to pick up on her absence, and that would put all of Valeria at risk.

No one, not even Glenrock and Naevia, the sprite and pixie Advisors to the Crown, knew that Elva had left Valeria for the world of its creator, Romira Royce; accompanied by his descendants, Rogue and Ranger. It was nerve wracking when Elva had been chosen to be the Guardian, but this was something else entirely. There were nights she didn't sleep at all, worrying after her daughter. Today would be a particularly hard day.

Evanna paused at the entry way, hearing the soft voices talking on the other side of the door. She took a deep breath before entering. "Evanna! Welcome!" Queen Eleria greeted her warmly. Naevia and Glenrock looked up from their places at the table, where they were analysing reports from their city officials.

"Good morning everyone," she answered.

"Hello Evanna," Glenrock said gruffly, a twinkle in his eye. "Get a bit lost this morning, did we?"

"No," she responded, forcing an airy smile. "I simply lost

track of time."

"Not a worry at all, Evanna," Naevia told her. "We've just been ordering our reports so we can provide city by city updates. Do you have yours?"

"Oh, yes!" She held up the scroll from under her arm. "Right here. Where should we start?"

"Let's start here and work our way south. Levindra's elves seem to be adjusting with minimal issues, though Vanya has informed me of a fight that broke out last week with some youths getting into a brawl with several sprites."

"Yes," Glenrock nodded gravely. "Whistler informed me of that. The lot of them were arrested, is that right?"

"Yes," Eleria confirmed. "But due to their age, counselling was given as the recommendation and I agree. There was always going to be teething issues; we knew this. The children who have always lived a certain way and haven't matured enough to understand the complexities of what a new world order means and lack the skills to express just what these changes mean for them," she continued. "We need to approach this with empathy and compassion or risk creating a greater divide."

"Yes, that seems fair," Glenrock agreed. "I would also recommend further education on the matter so they are not going into the world fresh out of school without any sort of exposure to the idea of equality," he suggested.

"Definitely. We'll inform the city officials so they can put the idea to the school heads," Naevia agreed. Queen Eleria nodded. "What say you, Evanna?"

Evanna shook her head slightly. "Yes! Absolutely. I feel that would rectify most, if not all, of the issues my officials have reported throughout a lot of the cities."

"Speaking of education," Eleria went on. "The Levindra Home of Community Relations is due to be finished this week and the children who have shown keen interest or skills in serving their communities as city officials are in the process of being transported here as we speak."

"That's wonderful!" Evanna responded. "I heard the sporting academy is finally finished its planning stage too. Do we have a name yet?"

"Not yet," Naevia responded. "The sheer number of students wishing to be considered for placement meant Fallon and Fillipe have gone into overdrive restructuring the building plans to accommodate for more dormitories," they said. "Ngarra, my Port Nixin official, has assisted them in locating three more coaches just yesterday based on the most recent reports."

"What's the location?"

"To the east, just outside the city limits. They set up on the edge of Lake Viridian to ensure access to water facilities."

"I'll be sure to send backup."

Once Levindra and North-East Point had been discussed, the Queen turned the conversation to the Observatory. She let

Glenrock and Naevia deliver their reports, which were minimal, before looking to Evanna.

"Yang Shi has said that life continues as normal from the discussions that have occurred at the meetings. Much like the other races at the Observatory, the academics tend to be more interested in getting on with the business of doing their jobs than worrying themselves with what's happening in the outside world. Nothing has changed at all, from what I can tell. Although…"

"What is it?" Queen Eleria pressed, concerned.

"Something is happening," Evanna said, exhaling heavily. "Ford is highly unresponsive and while I know we have our roles and I must focus on mine and let him do his, my role cannot be separated from who I am and having my husband keeping something from me is… distressing," she explained.

Eleria's face softened. "I understand," she said softly. "And I specifically chose to go last so I could enlighten you all on this very situation."

"What situation?" Glenrock barked roughly. "What has been kept from us?" Naevia also looked angry.

"As my official, Ford reported directly to me; just as any of your officials would report directly to each of you," she began. "This is our first meeting since the occurrence, and I am informing you in the appropriate forum. I have not actively hidden anything from any of you; I promise."

Glenrock and Naevia calmed, but Evanna still appeared

distressed. "Well then, what is it?"

"Last week, Ford was informed that Ariannah has been stirring." The revelation silenced the room. Then:

"How is that possible?"

"Elva put her to sleep herself! She insisted only *she* could wake her!"

"We must check on Elva immediately!"

"How many guards are watching her?"

"Ford has everything under control!" Eleria called over the top of them. "She is mumbling and shifting in her sleep as though she's dreaming. Based on his and the healers' observations, she is not waking up, but she is experiencing *something* within her mind. Elva's magic is keeping her asleep, but that's not stopping Ariannah from trying to wake."

"Elva could be in trouble. We must send a scout immediately!" Naevia demanded.

"I can guarantee that every effort will be made to ensure Elva's safety," the Queen insisted.

Evanna held back tears. *How could we possibly do that?*

CHAPTER 6

"Name and porpoise?"

§§

Elva's safety was definitely in question. The battle outside the carriage seemed to rage forever. The fear kept us tense and on edge, making it seem as though every moment took ten. None of us slept. I spent most of the time wondering just how long the seahorses could keep going. They'd been swimming at breakneck speed since the moment the Destroyer had been sighted.

"How long can Naira keep this up?" Rogue mumbled quietly.

"Naira is of the sea," Mortima said. "It will sustain them like nothing else can. It is why naiads are so highly valued in this work. You do not find a lot of them in the Centre. We are grateful to have Naira," he told us gravely. "They may very well determine whether or not we survive."

Shoal had been coming and going; allowing Maxima time to rest so her arms didn't seize up, circling the carriage to keep an eye on the battle, then coming inside to give us updates. On one such visit, he seemed triumphant. "Naira must be succeeding. We are outpacing the Destroyer. I can no longer see them on the horizon."

"How do we know Naira is ok?" I asked.

"Naira is battling the Destroyer," Mortima scoffed. "They are most definitely not ok, but they are alive. Had Naira died, it would have come for us by now. It certainly wouldn't be out of sight."

"SHOAL!" Maxima's voice railed from outside. He gave us a swift nod and pulled himself out through the window. He was back less than a minute later. "Naira is coming back!"

My breath caught in my throat, or the water did anyway. I felt like I didn't breathe for the entire time we were waiting for Naira's return. It was a full minute before we heard a dull *thunk* come from the front of the carriage.

It took another minute before the door opened again, but it wasn't Shoal who came through it; it was Maxima. She was breathing heavily as she collapsed onto the seat by her brother.

"What happened?"

"Is Naira ok?"

"Better condition than me right now!" Maxima gasped, her chest heaving as she massaged her upper arms. "I don't understand why the Destroyer wants you this badly! It's never pursued *anyone* like this before!" The three of us eyes each other warily, but didn't speak.

"Naira said it fled at dawn," she went on. "It completely disengaged and just disappeared. They feared it had attempted to circle around and so had tried to get back here as quickly as possible. Naira is very confused that after spending all day catching up to us, there's been no sign of it in their absence."

"So it went in a different direction?" I questioned. "Or it locked on to something else?"

"Either that or whatever controls it called it away," Mortima suggested.

"You think there's something controlling it?" Rogue asked.

"It makes sense. It behaves in a completely chaotic manner, then all of a sudden strikes a specific target with impunity?" Maxima said. "That behaviour doesn't make sense without something else pulling the strings."

That was an ominous thought to be left with. The remainder of the trip was despairingly slow and incredibly tense. At every moment we were waiting for another attack.

When we landed at the grand gates of Medina the following morning, it became clear our escort was glad to see the back of us. Naira was practically invisible in the morning light, Maxima having taken their place back in the driver's seat after the night's rest. "Good luck," Shoal said in a low growl, his red eyes staring us down suspiciously. "Whoever you are."

A guard met us at the gates. "Good morning," he greeted. "Ended up in the Centre, did we? Not smart, these days."

"So we learned," Elva agreed, her teeth clenched. He led us to the road that would take us to the palace. "Many more people here than in Valeria."

"Maybe," I said. "The pixies are so small their population could very easily add up to the same we're seeing here. It may just look busier." We swam among hundreds of others who were streaming towards the palace.

When it came into view, we all stopped short. "Wow!" Rogue gasped in amazement. It was enormous. Vast mounds of growing coral spiralled around each other to form high towers. At the very centre, corals of hundreds of different colours formed the main building.

We paused for only a moment, before pressing forward with the crowd. It took almost an hour before we were through the front doors and being seated in a large hall. Two mermaids and a cecaelian were swimming around with clipboards, asking for names and the reason for them being here. Triakis of all types stood at every doorway, watching the proceedings; a shell shield in one hand, a carved coral spear in the other.

"Well this looks familiar," Rogue said, gesturing to the workers with the clipboards. "The Marble Palace did exactly the same."

"What do you know?" I asked Elva. "Can you see what the

royals are like?"

"Romira expected the leading families of his worlds to welcome their people always," she said. "To ensure they always kept the world's needs as the highest priority. I assume every palace will have a similar process.

"I can't see them specifically, but they're not a royal family," she continued. "They have a Lord and Lady here. They don't govern the way Eleria did; or the way it does now."

We nodded as we watched the secretaries slowly move along the lines of people waiting. If the visitor was deemed important, they were assigned a guard, who placed them in a queue to see the Lord and Lady. If not, they were given an appointment for a later date and sent home.

When a pink Mermaid with long brown hair and a clipboard was four people away from us, Elva turned to Rogue and me. She seemed anxious again. "What's our story?" she asked. "We can't say 'Hey, we're from another world and want to see the Lord and Lady so we can find the Guardian and *take the Heart of Mattara*'. What do we do?" She seemed slightly hysterical. Rogue grabbed her hand and squeezed to quiet her down.

I smiled at her and shook my head. "It's all right," I began. "We just tell them that we have urgent news for the Lord and Lady about the Guardian and will only tell them directly."

"Works every time," Rogue told her.

"*Once*," Elva retorted, panicked. "Maximum, it worked

once."

"Name and porpoise?" the pink Mermaid asked brightly, not looking up from her clipboard.

"*What~?*"

"~Hello!" Rogue cut me off. "My name is… River and this is my sister Kenna and our friend Elva," she lied quickly, before getting up and whispering. "We have news for the Lord and Lady of Mattara… It's about the Guardian," she paused and watched as the mermaid's pink face grew pinker and her eyes widen.

"Follow me," she ordered, before swimming away swiftly, clicking her fingers. We were instantly flanked by two massive triakin guards. I started to get scared. What had we gotten ourselves into?

We followed her as quickly as the guards allowed, through the crowd of people coming and going, and into a corridor off the giant entrance. We were led to a large second set of doors at the end. On the other side was a massive hall. I swam with Rogue and Elva on my left and bowed to the Lord and Lady as directed by the mermaid.

"Why have these cecaelia been brought to us this day?" the Lady asked. She was a short, lime green Mermaid, with seaweed ravelled through her hair. Her eyes were dark and her lips were pale.

"Lord Morgan and Lady Oceana." The pink mermaid bowed low. "They claim to have news of your daughter, the

Lady Marina, Your Highnesses," she told them.

THEIR DAUGHTER?

"Our daughter?" The Lord repeated my thoughts out loud. He was a tall merman with shoulder length, black hair and brown eyes. His tail was wide and as dark as his hair and he too, had seaweed tangled through it.

"What news do you bring?" Lady Oceana asked, rising from her chair and gesturing for their escort mermaid to leave. The three of us swam up the stairs and stood beside the Lord and Lady, both of whom had risen from their seats. "What news?" Lady Oceana said again.

"The Guardian is your daughter?" Rogue questioned, frowning.

"Who are you?" the Lord asked Rogue suspiciously. "Everybody in all of Mattara knows who our daughter is!"

"We're not from Mattara," I told him. "And I'm sorry, but we have no news."

Lord Morgan and Lady Oceana became angry. "Who are you?" he repeated, his face like stone.

I took a deep breath, not sure what to say. *Will they believe we're the real Rogue and Ranger? What if they don't? What do we do?* I knew I had to say something, but I didn't know what. Typical of me, I completely froze and said nothing.

"My name is Elva," Elva stepped forward and bowed to the Lord and Lady. "And I am the Guardian of the Heart of

Valeria. My friends are the descendants of the creator of your world… and mine; Romira Royce."

"What?" Lady Oceana gasped. "My daughter is the Guardian!"

"Of the Heart of Mattara, yes," Rogue said. "The Heart of Valeria; the Heart of Truth, is another; both pieces of a whole."

Elva stepped forward and touched the locket at her neck. The elf appeared to stir as the Heart pulsed pink inside. The Lord and Lady gasped as the light washed over them. "There are seven in total. They must be reunited."

Lady Oceana drew back, terror on her face. She looked to her husband, who held her close protectively. "My name is Ranger," I said gently. "This is my sister, Rogue. Romira Royce was our ancestor. We were sent for the Heart of Mattara."

CHAPTER 7

Morgana

§§

"Should we just leave?"

"There's no point. These people are our only connection to Marina. We can't leave until they tell us her location."

"I'm certain I can find her with my piece of the Heart."

"Maybe, but it could take ten times as long."

"We're wasting that much time as it is!"

"We just need to hold out for a little bit longer."

I listened to Rogue and Elva go back and forth, unable to join in. They both had perfectly valid and reasonable arguments and I couldn't tell which route we should take to continue. I hated having to choose, so I sat there silently, listening to the exchange.

We had been whisked away by guards and taken to a room at the very top of the palace. We'd been alone for almost an hour. I remembered so easily because after ten minutes I started watching the clock, wondering how a clock could work underwater.

Life with Elva changed things for us. It had always been Rogue and me. Sure there were mutual friends we had, like Gia, but usually I kept to myself and Rogue did the group things. We were practically living with Elva now and we were needing to consider her in everything we did where we never had to before and if all went as planned, there would be more Guardians coming.

I never did well around other people. The pretending I did in Valeria and now here in Mattara was like play acting around normal people at home, so it was almost easy here, and the behavioural expectations weren't the same as home so I felt I could relax more.

At least I did… As I sat there on the window frame, overlooking the city, the idea of being surrounded by a group of people who were pivotal to saving my home and theirs was terrifying. What if I said the wrong thing and hurt their feelings? What if I upset them and they refused to help us? *And the more Guardians and Hearts we collect the more likely that is to happen!*

The coral clock had just ticked over to a new hour when a door to our right flew open and a pale blue, slim mermaid with long blonde waves of hair entered, followed closely by three triakin guards, all slimmer and sleeker than the ones we'd seen downstairs. The mermaid's eyes were wide; a bright blue. Her tail was almost white, but opalescent and her frilly fin was transparent. She seemed angry and anxious.

"Who are you?" she demanded to know.

"Rogue, Ranger and Elva," Rogue answered. "Who are you?"

"I am Lady Morgana; not only sister, but twin to Lady Marina, the Guardian of the Heart of Mattara," she answered fiercely. "And I was informed of who you three are; I simply did not believe it."

"Sounds familiar," I muttered under my breath.

"And now what do you believe?" Elva asked, getting up and touching her hand to the Guardian necklace. Her tentacles melted away and left her with her mermaid tail once more. Rogue and I followed suit.

Morgana choked back a scream. "H-how?"

"It's part of who we are," Rogue answered. "Romira's worlds are in danger; *all* of them. We need to find your sister."

"There are *others?*"

"Many others," I told her. "Elva comes from one of them."

"In Valeria, home of the Fae," Elva said. "I am a Guardian too."

Lady Morgana waved at the guards. "Leave us." They nodded and left the room, gently closing the door behind them. "This 'Heart' you claim to have…" she said, breathing in deeply. "May I see it?"

Elva opened the locket around her neck and the pulsing

pink Heart it held began to glow brighter. The pink deepened until it was almost red. None of us had ever known it to glow so bright.

"What's happening?" I asked, shielding my eyes.

"It usually only does this to warn of danger. I think it senses the Mattara Heart," Elva explained, her eyes opening again in an attempt to see through the glow. "I knew it could; from the moment we arrived I could feel it, but I didn't think it would alert us to it until we were near the Guardian."

"You… are," Morgana told us slowly. "You are linked to Marina through the Heart you carry… and through me."

"What do you mean?" I asked her, frowning.

"Marina and I are identical twins… Rare. From birth I could always sense where she was. Neither of us were ever lost, or alone," she started, drifting towards the window facing the north of Medina and gazing out of it.

I thought about how much it would hurt to be apart from Rogue for an extended period of time; how hard it was at the times we had been apart so far in life. If one of us were to take a position that separated us forever? The very idea was unimaginable. There were times when I believed I could almost hear Rogue's thoughts. I could tell with an almost scientific accuracy what she was feeling most of the time, but to actually *know* without it being mostly my intuition was a level of twinning Rogue and I had never achieved.

Morgana continued to stare out of the window, holding

her hands. "I know where she is. She's far away right now, so all I get is intense feelings, or the odd image. Sometimes she sends me messages. Not often though; she feels it is abusing the power of the Heart of Peace to do so. But… I can tell that she knows you're here and who you are. She wants to see you."

My heart leapt. She could hear us right now. She wanted to see us. "Will she give us the Heart?" Elva cut through my thoughts, pulling me out of my waking dream.

"That, I can't tell you," Morgana replied, turning back to us. "All I know is that she wants to hear what you have to say, in person." She crossed the room and opened the doors. "Please ready Baylene for departure," she requested. "We leave as soon as she is ready."

"*We?*" I repeated.

"Yes," Morgana replied matter of factly. "You'll never find her without me; and I won't miss a chance to be reunited with my sister, no matter how little a time it is for." We exited the room and headed through what we learned was Coral Palace. It was a wonderfully colourful place, with plant life of every hue covering the walls and floor. As we swam down a flight of redundant stairs, Morgana continued to talk. "You are Elva, the Guardian of the Heart of… what was it again?" she asked, as she led us through the palace kitchens.

"The Heart of Truth," she answered, nodding. "I am of Valeria."

"And what lives in this *world* of yours?" she went on. "Are the waters warm?"

Elva chuckled. "We don't live in water there. We live on the land. We *have* water; a lake, rivers and streams. We have elves, fairies, sprites and pixies," Elva told her.

"Land… yes," Morgana said softly. "I've seen it in some of the pictures I see in Marina's head. Before she became the Guardian, *land* was mythology. Something kids read about in stories of fantastical lands and unheard of creatures." She paused for a moment. "What are you?"

"I am half elf, half fairy," she answered.

Morgana gasped, her eyes widening. "Never have I heard of such a thing! Is that why you were chosen?"

"I was chosen because I was the best person for the job," she replied harshly. "It was meant to be me."

"How was your sister chosen?" I asked curiously. "What happened to the Guardian she took over from?"

Morgana paled, suddenly looking very sullen. "The previous Guardian, was a cecaelia previously known as Liang. They had lived to the absolute age. No matter how old Liang became, it seemed they would never pass."

"The 'absolute age'? What's that?"

"The age for passing into the void should you survive all the standard dangers of living," she answered. "Attack, illness and so on. No one had ever been known to live beyond this age before."

"How old is the absolute age?"

"It isn't an actual number. It is the time when you have fulfilled your life's true purpose."

I considered the idea. "So as the Guardian, it was like their purpose would never be fulfilled so long as the Heart needed them."

"Does that mean Liang was your first and only Guardian before your sister?" Elva asked.

"No, there have been many, all of them living to a standard age," Morgana sighed. "No one knows why Liang was living as long as they were, but the Heart *had* to move on, so Mother and Father planned the inauguration, invited Liang here to Medina, and had them choose the new Guardian."

"Wait, *Liang* chose your sister?" Rogue said. "Not the Heart?"

"Well of *course* the Heart chose!" Morgana laughed, waving her hand dismissively. "It just used Liang to *do* it. It glowed for Marina, just like it had for Liang at *their* inauguration.

"Mother and Father were so mad," she continued, shaking her head at the thought. She talked as though she hadn't had anyone to talk to for a long time. Knowing how I was with Rogue, I imagined I'd be the same if someone was interested in talking to me after so long being without her.

"They never knew she'd put herself forth for consideration, you see? They were up in the stands, watching all of the participants, but she was hearing a headdress and mask so they never saw her face.

"Liang slowly walked down the line of people, and one by one, they left if the Heart didn't shine for them. Marina was the last in line," she told us animatedly. "We almost thought nothing had happened. She turned to leave as well, but right as she went to move, the Heart started to glow! The rest is history!

"Mother and Father were *horrified* when they saw it was her, because had the people known it was her and she *hadn't* been chosen, it would have been *highly* embarrassing for them. But, she was chosen and then revealed herself; the people cheered and though it was only proper for the leaders of Mattara to also be committed to protecting the Heart of Peace, even if it meant risking their own lives. It caused quite a stir on the tides, it did. Mother and Father were thrilled once they saw how happy the public were with them because of it."

It didn't seem right. The Heart wasn't meant to work that way. I could tell Rogue felt the same. Elva was frowning, touching the Heart of Valeria for comfort. If the life expectancy here was based on fulfilling life's true purpose, then Liang still living meant their job wasn't finished. They shouldn't have passed on the Heart before it was ready. "Is Liang still alive?"

"No," she sighed. "We *begged* them to stay here with us,

for their protection, of course. No Guardian had ever lived long enough to no longer be a Guardian before. We knew they would be in danger if left alone. Liang refused; our offer, our guards, even an escort to their new residence, wherever that was. They were killed within the month. It was quite distressing"

Once on the other side of the kitchens, the staff having been given a very detailed list for the journey, we were led into a large chamber that could only be the palace library. It was lined with hundreds of thousands of books. Maps of every city papered the walls, and on a large pedestal in the centre of the large, open room on the main floor of the library was a map of Mattara in detail.

"You will find my sister, Lady Marina, here," Morgana began, pointing to the western edge of Mattara.

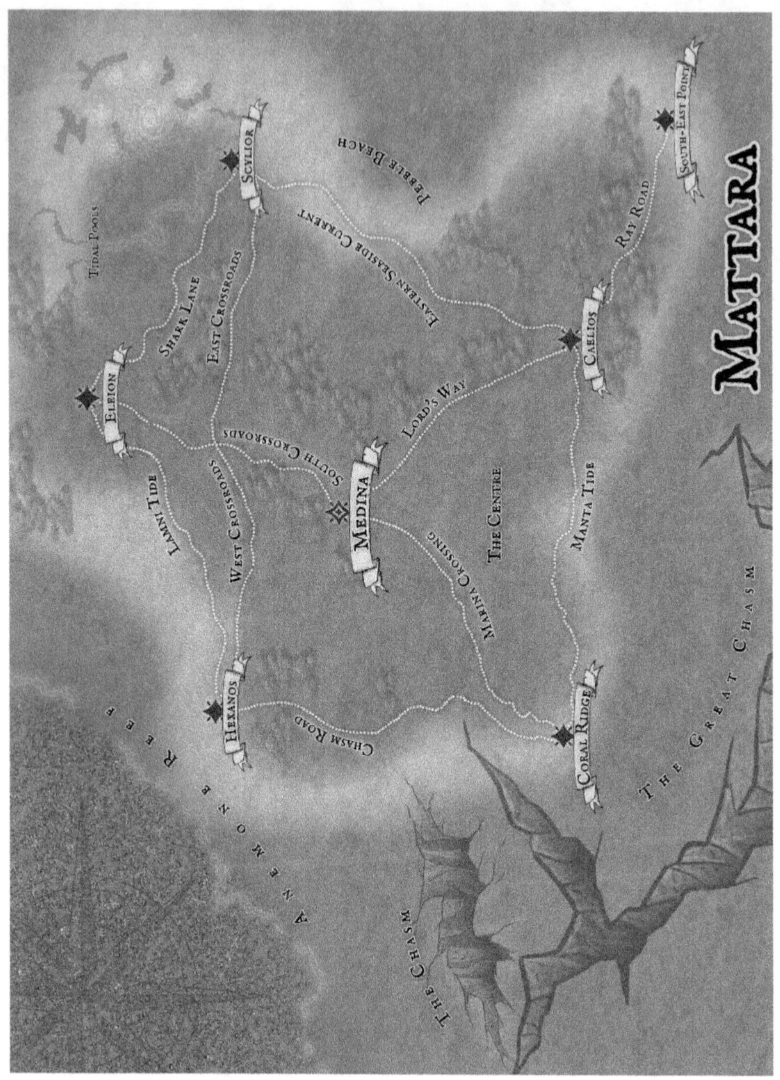

"The Great Chasm?" Elva read. "Sounds promising."

"I know," Morgana replied, frowning. "It's a horrible place; incredibly dangerous. I didn't want her to go there, but she insisted that she would be the safest there, *because* of that danger, and that she would be fine because the Heart would protect her."

"It does make sense. As the Guardian I had to find a dangerous place that either none could find or none would risk. It was the easiest way to make sure no one would steal the Heart."

"What can we expect in this *Great Chasm?*" I asked.

"A large number of carnivorous fish, some whales migrate there as well," Morgana answered thoughtfully. "The biggest risk are the shellfish… or feral naiads."

"I'm sorry, what?" Rogue questioned.

"There are naiads who choose to live down in the Great Chasm, in order to avoid mer life. As beings of pure water, they can find life outside their cities of Eleion and Potame rather fast. It's slower and quieter there, but, when they remove themselves for so long, they become unfeeling, more animalistic. They can get quite violent if you get too close, which is easy to accidentally do when you can't see them," she snorted.

A cold, hard lump grew in my throat. Avoiding society turns you into a monster, huh? It became clear that this was going to be much more dangerous than Valeria.

CHAPTER 8
The Sea-nic Route

§§

It took far too long to prepare for the journey to the Great Chasm. Morgana insisted that everything had to be perfect and that Baylene, whoever that was, had to be ready to come with us. "Only I know where she is and I cannot disclose her location willingly. It is part of the magic of the Heart," she explained.

We had spent days in Medina, while Morgana trivialised over every minute detail. She seemed far more focused on a fun visit to her sister than the actual reason we were going; the potential destruction of multiple worlds. When this was brought up, however, she seemed to ignore it entirely, insisting that "Marina will fix everything!" Rogue seemed about ready to rip her tail off and throw it at her.

Morgana's parents, the Lord and Lady of Mattara, seemed nowhere to be seen. They hadn't made an appearance since our first day in Medina. Morgana ignored this too. "Oh, Mother and Father always have events happening. It's all luncheon this and charity ball that. They never stay still, my parents."

"Even when it involves their daughter?" Rogue pushed. "Who they haven't seen in… How long has she been the Guardian?"

"Twelve years."

"They haven't seen her in *twelve years* and now we show up and they're completely AWOL? They are *still* more focused on food and dancing?"

"What can I say?" Morgana shrugged. "They're good leaders, and when Marina was here they were very good parents to the both of us. Once she was chosen, they just considered us adults who could take care of ourselves. The public love them and they do whatever they can to keep it that way. Their image is very important to them." I had shaken my head in disbelief, both at how the leaders of the world of Mattara were behaving and at their daughter's seemingly oblivious reaction to it.

Now, we were finally leaving, after one of the triakin guards had informed us that the mysterious *Baylene* was finally ready. Morgana bustled around us excitedly. "It's time!"

"How do we get there?" Rogue asked, pulling on the pack Morgana had given her.

"We travel along the Marina, or Guardian crossing, to Coral Ridge," she replied. "The Great Chasm is a tourist attraction and has many carriages that travel there each week. Should we miss one, the next comes three days later. Otherwise, we can get seahorses to ride, or stay with Baylene," she waved an arm and shrugged. "We'll play it by ear. It'll take about a week, depending on how Baylene feels. She tends to move slower during mating season."

Elva started choking on the water around her. "Excuse me?" But Morgana was already gone. We followed her through the main foyer of the Coral Palace and into the grand courtyard out front, where a humpback whale was waiting for us, a basket of woven seagrass tied to its back.

"Oh!" I gasped, before starting to laugh. "Baylene! Ha!"

"Oh, that makes sense," Rogue said, nodding sagely.

"This is Baylene!" Morgana introduced happily. "She is my *best* friend, after Marina of course." Morgana hugged her around the neck. Baylene crooned almost mournfully in response. "She's not fully grown yet, barely a teenager in whale terms, but definitely big enough to take us to Marina. All aboard!"

I swam up and settled into the basket atop Baylene, my pack by my side. Elva sat beside me. "So… is it mating season or no?" she asked Morgana nervously.

♠

Along the road to Coral Ridge were many villages, all of which were ecstatic to see their Lady. We were welcomed by many families and asked to stay by all of them. Every village was the same routine, but we didn't have time to waste. Morgana was insistent that we not be rude, for it was rare these villages were visited by any members of her family. She was also determined to show each of the villagers how honoured she felt by their hospitality, by spending hours upon hours with them each time. By the third village, the 'week or so' Morgana had promised had already disappeared.

There was one thing that had caught my eye in the first and second villages, which kept me on the lookout throughout the following days. It began at sunset on our first day. We'd just reached the first village; a small town called Mantra just off the main road.

While Morgana's swarm of well wishers whisked her away to the dining hall, I noticed that one man, a triakis, swam the other way, a hard, determined look on his face. I thought it strange that with a young, beautiful Lady coming to your village, a young man wouldn't be falling all over her. This man was literally going in the opposite direction.

"Maybe he's taken?" Elva shrugged when I mentioned it to her. I nodded, but I was still left with my gut telling me something was amiss.

My unease grew deeper at the next town, the following

day. Once again, Morgana was speaking to the villagers, who were doting upon her, and once again, I saw the face in the crowd. "It's the triakis!" I hissed to Elva and Rogue.

"Shoal?" Rogue piped up, looking around with sudden interest. "Where?" They looked around through the crowd and turned back to me.

"Not *Shoal!* The man from the village yesterday!"

"Where?"

"There!" But he'd already disappeared. They looked to where I was pointing, but there was nothing to see.

"Ranger, are you sure it was~?" Rogue began.

"~Yes, I'm sure!" I snapped.

I swam away and as I came around the back of a house, saw a black shark tail turn the corner just ahead of me. "I don't think so," I growled low. I shot after him, flying around the corner as fast as my tail could take me. I was in another alley. I swam around the next corner and found myself on a busy street. I groaned and smacked my hands on my tail. I'd lost him… and now I was lost.

♠

"We didn't *see* him!" Elva whined when I finally found them again. "If we did, of *course* we would have come with you!" We were in our hosts' home, Baylene grazing in the kelp fields outside our window.

"The point is I *did* see him!" I yelled back. "If you were any sort of friend, you would have given me the benefit of the doubt!" Elva shrank back, stung. Rogue hadn't said a word. She felt horrible, but I wasn't letting up. I was always the one dismissed and now of all times, when there was such a high risk for everyone involved, I was still just thought to be causing an unwanted fuss.

"What's going on?" Morgana had entered the room.

"Nothing," I answered quickly, leaving through the opposite door, letting it slam behind me. I didn't want her to know about the triakis I'd seen. I didn't want to scare her. It could lead to her wanting to return to the castle instead of taking us to the Great Chasm, which was the priority at this point. This meant keeping her alive to get us there, and I was starting to worry that it wasn't us he was stalking, it was Morgana. Or worse, that it was the Destroyer trying to find its way to Marina as well.

After a night of restless sleep and dreams of faceless men and being eaten alive by sharks, we moved on. Every village we came to along the road to Coral Ridge, I saw the same triakis, but the others didn't. I kept telling myself it's because they weren't looking, but after a while, even I started to doubt. I searched every face and with every village, I swore that I saw the one I was looking for, but was I really?

I stopped speaking to Elva, Rogue and Morgana entirely. I found I couldn't. Every time I considered trying, I was paralysed, unsure of what to say, or how to express my feelings. I knew I would sound crazy if I pushed it, but I also didn't want them to dismiss it if I told them that maybe I had been seeing him because I was specifically looking for something to see.

While Rogue was sorry for what happened at the second town, she still hadn't seen the man since the first village. Elva was still grumbling about what I'd said to her, which scared me, because if she decided to go home, it would be my fault. Then it would all be over.

Morgana remained oblivious to the whole situation. The only thing she was interested in was Elva. She asked her a hundred questions a day while we were travelling.

"Is cross breeding common in your World?" she asked. "What were your parents? How long do your kind live? What's it like to live in the open air? What powers did you have as the Guardian? What can your Heart do? What will happen when your Heart joins with Marina's? Elves are immortal, right? If they are, why is it that your world doesn't over-populate?" It got annoying after a while, but it wasn't every day you met someone from another world, and Elva seemed happy to answer her questions as best she could.

This all changed just after we left the last village. Coral Ridge was finally in sight and the main road was bare all the way to the city. "From its uppermost tower… we're about an hour away," Morgana informed us.

I had been watching again, as I had for every trip between the villages. At the very moment she told us we were close to city, I saw something in the corner of my eye. I spun around to face the way we had come and my breath caught in my chest with a loud gasp.

"What is it?" Rogue asked, alarmed.

"*It's the stalker! The Triakis!*" I screamed, watching him swim through the water with an incredible speed. "SWIM! *Go! Go now!*"

CHAPTER 9
The Destroyer

§§

"**B**ut Baylene!" Morgana cried out in distress.

"I HIGHLY DOUBT HE WANTS THE WHALE, MORGANA!" We were all swimming as fast as we could. Morgana had turned and seen who was following us, screaming a word that was so completely inaudible, she had to repeat herself as we fled for our lives.

"*Destroyer!*" she screeched again as she swam. My heart seemed to stop. That, or time itself did. The Destroyer had finally tracked us down, and it knew we were headed for the Guardian; why else would it be trying so hard to reach us?

The city gates were wide open. We were within range. All of us began calling out to the guards. It wasn't until we were a few feet away that they heard what we were yelling and recognised Morgana.

"*Close the gates!* she ordered, her face hard as we crossed the threshold. *"It's the Destroyer!"* The guards had a strange look cross their face, as though they were confused, but they were loyal soldiers and heeded their Lady. They both nodded and pushed the doors closed. Morgana pulled all three guards around to face her directly.

"Listen to me carefully," she demanded. "When it demands entry, you have to let it in, or it will destroy the city to do so, but you must delay it as much as you can. We *must* escape. Have the stableman bring us your four fastest seahorses." One of the three guards swam off, but the other two remained, both listening intently to Morgana's words.

"Try to keep it distracted; it will attempt to maintain its face to keep as low a profile as possible. Pretend not to know it is the Destroyer; act as casually as you can unless your life is threatened. If loses his temper, let him leave, but you *must* stall him for as long as possible while we get away. Do not fight for me; we of the High Family can protect ourselves," she finished as the third guard returned with the seahorses; a deep purple, a bright yellow, a fiery red and a liquid black.

The three guards bowed to Morgana before we all mounted our steeds. My seahorse's black scales glinted in the afternoon sunlight as I took the reins, which were inscribed: Night Light. Rogue was upon the red, Elva on the purple and Morgana on the yellow, which immediately began to rear and snort before she held her hand to its neck and closed her eyes.

"Calm yourself," she whispered. The seahorse skittered

slightly before it settled, then we were off. It took an agonisingly long time to reach the other side of the city and the southern gates. Once we had, the gates flew open and we sped out onto the open sands of the western sea.

The gates closed behind us and as we urged our steeds on, the need to go faster overpowering everything else in my mind. Every moment I felt the Destroyer closing in on us. It was like an intense pressure weighing down, getting heavier by the minute. The Centre had felt similar, but this was infinitely stronger. As my heart raced faster than the seahorses, I urged Night Light on.

We'd been fleeing for our lives for almost a half hour when a loud roar broke through the sound of the blood rushing in my ears. "I DID NOT AGREE TO THIS WHEN I CAME WITH YOU!" Elva screamed.

"*And what contract do you think we signed?*" Rogue yelled back.

There was another vicious roar. I couldn't take it anymore. I looked back. The jet black tail with the silver streak along the fin; it was the triakis; the Destroyer. It was close; too close.

"FOLLOW ME!" Rogue suddenly cried. She veered to the right, heading for a large field of long seaweed. I shot towards it, passing Elva and Morgana and leaping into the slimy growths. Night Light pushed his way through it with great speed, but Elva's steed was just as fast. We swam together, neck and neck, as we flew through the forest of weeds.

"Ew, ew, ew," she kept on repeating, shaking the slimy tendrils from her shoulders.

"Where's Morgana?" I called to her.

"Right behind me!" she yelled back to me over the rush of the water.

The pressure lifted for a brief moment as we flew across a large clearing in the centre of the seaweed grove. Just as quickly as it appeared, it was gone, as we shot right across it. We had pressed on through the seaweed field on the other side of the clearing when another roar came from behind us. "Faster," I hissed desperately to Night Light, but he was already being pushed to the limit.

As Rogue flashed in and out of sight in front of us, and Elva and me thundered on side by side, we continued to call out to one another. "Lady! Are you alright?" I called out to Morgana, not looking back. "Lady Morgana! Answer me!"

She didn't. Everything was silent; utterly, terrifyingly silent. The Destroyer had ceased its roaring. Lady Morgana still didn't respond; that was until the loudest roar yet split through the water, followed by a high pitched scream and a gurgling cry.

My body froze up, stopping Night Light in his tracks and almost sending me over his neck. In front of me, Elva and Rogue had also stopped. Without a moment's wait or a single word to each other, we turned and sped back the way we had come, all need for stealth lost as we swam over the top of the seaweed to get there with all haste.

In a matter of seconds, the clearing had come into view and we were diving for it. We hit the ground, all of us coming out of our saddles. Lady Morgana was on the ground; a silver dagger speared through her heart. Holding her head was the triakis… the Destroyer.

"TELL ME WHERE SHE IS!" it was screaming at her. The male form the Destroyer had taken was dark eyed. His hair was short and brown, and his face burned with anger.

She didn't answer. After a gurgling sound from the back of her throat, she went very still. Without warning her body exploded into darkness. We stood there, stunned, unsure of what was happening. When the inky blackness abated, Lady Morgana's body was gone.

The moment the Destroyer saw us, it was off the ground and gone. There was only a split second's hesitancy, before: "AFTER IT!" Rogue bellowed, pulling herself back into the saddle.

"Wait!" Elva yelled, but she went unheard. I followed Rogue's lead, leaping onto Night Light and pelting after the Destroyer as fast as he could carry me.

Morgana was gone. Because of us, a Lady of the world of Mattara, and our only way to find the Guardian of the Heart of Peace, was dead. We'd failed, but we weren't going to let the Destroyer get away with what it had done to her.

We sped after him with all our mounts could give, back over the seaweed fields and on towards the Great Chasm. We pushed on faster, and faster. The Destroyer was in our sights, as was a small, hollowed out village in ruins off to the left.

As soon as we could see him, he disappeared into it. We kept going. Nothing was going to stop us from avenging Morgana. Elva, Rogue and I were enough to defeat Ariannah and we'd make sure it was enough now.

Through my rage, I began to think. *Why is it fleeing? Something isn't right. The Destroyer can fight harder than any other being in this world. It's destroyed villages and towns; wrought utter destruction in multiple cities; taken countless people. If it can get rid of us in a single move, why is it running? This could be a trap. Why else would it flee to a ruined village?*

I couldn't believe how angry I was, but things weren't adding up, and confusion was starting to dilute my anger. Rogue and me had brought Elva here. All of us were intruders in Mattara and the Destroyer had been waiting for us. It was our presence that had killed the Lady. It was our fault; my fault. We had to make sure we didn't make any more mistakes.

"Where did it go?" Rogue asked, looking around aggressively.

"Stop!" Elva hissed. She seemed agitated and scared. She was clasping the locket at her neck, which was glowing feebly. Elva was clearly weakening. As Rogue and Ranger, we were a part of all Venturan worlds, and as a Royce creation, Elva could live in our world easily, but this was not her world, or ours. She couldn't last for much longer.

"It'll be around. It wants us here for a reason," I whispered ominously. "Rogue, something isn't right."

"You're not *thinking!*" Elva insisted, frustrated.

"What do you mean?" Rogue snapped. "It killed Morgana! There's nothing to think about!"

"The Destroyer has been described as an all powerful being and you think it needs to *swim* to escape us?" Elva started. "You think it would keep a simple triakin body when it was capable of fighting Naira for as long as it did with no form at all?"

Rogue paused. I exhaled, trying to force myself to calm down. "She's not wrong, Rogue. It *is* odd that this creature would target Morgana, but not us. We know the Destroyer would jump at the chance get rid of us, but instead it swam away?"

"Maybe it wants Marina *more!*" Rogue growled. "It's easier to find her with us alive. This way," she said harshly. Typical Rogue. There would be no way of getting to her now.

I exchanged a glance with Elva before following Rogue. We walked through the deserted town, skirting the square. It was like a maze, with all roads leading back to the middle, where a large cecaelian statue stood in the pride of place.

We moved silently, making no noise for the sake of our mission. Whoever this triakis was, Destroyer or not, it had killed Morgana, and there was a reckoning to be had.

There was a movement to my left. I paused and listened. There was the distinct sound of a closing door. I caught the girls' attention. "That way," I mouthed.

I circled the house. The door was hanging off its hinges. Dismounting, I tied the reins to a post around the corner and edged my way into the house, Elva and Rogue behind me. A large doorway was directly in front of us. It led to what had been the living room. We peered around the corner and finding no one, ventured inside. A noise came from the door opposite. Standing rigidly beside the entrance, I managed a look inside.

It was sitting at the kitchen table, still looking like a triakis. There appeared to be a wound in its side. *Good. It was by Morgana's body when it exploded and it probably got hurt.* We had to act quickly.

I pulled a rope from over Rogue's shoulder and in an instant, stormed the room and tackled the triakis to the ground. As I had hoped, it was weak enough for us to tie it up without using magic to release itself.

"WHAT ARE YOU DOING?" it roared. It struggled in the chair it was bound to but appeared incapable of escape.

"*Why?*"

"WHY WHAT?" it roared again.

"Why the Lady?" Rogue hissed, pulling a dagger from her bag and holding to the creature's neck. "If you were after us, why kill Morgana?"

"I WASN'T AFTER YOU!" it continued to rage, struggling against the bonds, but wincing from the pain.

"*We* are Rogue and Ranger!" I yelled at it. "We were who you were sent after, but you got the wrong person!"

"*I wasn't sent after anybody!*" the creature screamed. "I WENT AFTER IT BECAUSE IT *KIDNAPPED* HER!"

"Don't bother lying to us. We know who you are. You've been stalking us since we left the palace in Medina," Rogue growled. "You're the Destroyer."

Its face changed, but it didn't seem angry at being found out. On the contrary; it seemed confused. "I'm not the Destroyer," the triakis said softly. "I killed the Destroyer."

"*You're a liar!*" Rogue hissed. "You came after us, but got Morgana instead! You *failed* to kill us and now you're covering yourself in order to get another chance!"

"No…" Elva whispered in astonishment. "He speaks the truth."

"How can you tell?"

The Heart around her neck pulsed twice, before dying down. The Heart of Truth. Valerians upheld honesty as their highest value. Elva could sense the truth, we'd always known that, but surely the Destroyer would have ways to circumvent that. *It's all about power. Is the power of Romira's Heart of*

Truth enough to combat Raphael's Destroyer?

I turned to what we believed to be the Destroyer, the doubt growing even stronger than before. Elva was here for a reason. There would be no point of bringing her here if we were only going to ignore her advice and what she believed. "What do we do, Elva?" I asked her.

She exhaled. She'd obviously been holding it for a while. She stepped towards the triakis and let the pink light of the Valerian Heart wash over him. "Tell us a story, triakis," she said softly and the pink light paled slightly.

He turned away from us. After struggling slightly, he went limp. He then looked back up to us and sighed. "I'm not getting out of this am I?" he asked gruffly.

"No."

"Will that locket be able to tell you whether or not I'm lying?" he went on.

"Yes."

Rogue and I stood back during Elva and the triakis' exchange. After a few moments of silence, he took a deep breath and sighed. "My name is Mannix," he began. "Lady Morgana is my fiancée."

CHAPTER 10

Back to School

§§

"What?" Rogue snapped at him. She was silenced by a look from Elva.

"About six weeks ago," he began. "I noticed a change in her. She wasn't the same. She was distant and cold. I didn't understand what was happening, until I noticed that she stopped speaking to Marina."

"What do you mean?" I asked him.

"Morgana and Marina are linked. They can speak to each other through their minds. They spoke every night… until she changed. I noticed that they weren't speaking, then I realised why."

"Morgana said she could only get images or vague feelings from Marina," I interjected. "That occasionally she would send messages but chose not to abuse the magic of the Heart."

"It *wasn't* Morgana," Mannix growled in a low voice. "It lied. Morgana would talk to her all the time; out loud. I would hear half the conversation from our end. This *creature* didn't because it *couldn't.* Morgana couldn't contact Marina because they weren't linked anymore. They weren't linked anymore because Morgana *wasn't* Morgana anymore," he finished with a whisper.

"The Destroyer had taken her," Elva breathed.

Mannix nodded and took a shuddering breath as he fought whatever was happening in his head. "As soon as it knew I suspected, I was ejected from the palace and the engagement was called off. I was marked as a traitor and forced to flee," he went on. "When I learned that the Destroyer was finally on the move, I hastened to follow. You see, I didn't kill Morgana… I killed the Destroyer."

"The black smoke…" Rogue mumbled, a dawning look of realisation on her face.

"Well, after I stabbed it in the heart, it couldn't exactly bleed, could it?" he shot back. "It wasn't a creature of flesh and bone like us!"

"And cartilage," I put in unhelpfully. Rogue rolled her eyes. "'Tell me where she is'…" I said, repeating what Mannix had cried out as the Destroyer died in his arms.

"It had to put her somewhere," he said desperately, shaking his head. "I just don't know where! And now… I never will." Elva rushed to untie Mannix as he hung there limply. He jumped slightly as she came into contact but stopped moving when he saw what she was doing.

"Could the Destroyer possibly have a lair in the Great Chasm?" I asked suddenly. Mannix looked down to his wound as it was uncovered. "That's where it was taking us, saying that was where Marina was, and I'm guessing it didn't even know where she was to begin with… so what else would be at the Great Chasm but Morgana?"

"Death," he coughed. "The Great Chasm is home to Mattara's largest shellfish. The shells are attached to the rock at its base and the tentacles can almost reach the top of the Chasm. Anything they can reach… is devoured." Elva pulled away from him as the ropes floated away, the Heart glowing brighter. She touched the wound in his side and he cried out as the muscle and skin knitted itself together.

"I can't do a lot here, but I can still do that!" she said with smug satisfaction. Mannix grabbed at the place where the wound had been, looking between it and Elva, a stunned look on his face.

"What a fate that would have been," I mumbled dramatically. "Eaten alive by giant shellfish." It scared me to know how willingly we had almost gone to our deaths. A lot made sense now. All of Morgana's questions to Elva… and the fact that in Coral Ridge, she was referring to Mannix as 'he' instead of 'it', as one generally spoke of the Destroyer, for it could obviously take on any form. All of it left a hard, sick feeling in my stomach. I shivered.

"The Destroyer's power is based in the Centre," Rogue

reminded us. "That's why Anomar wanted us gone so badly…
I think it's time we paid her another visit."

♠

It took almost a week to get back to the Centre. We made our
way back to Chasm Road and instead of following it, crossed
it completely and into the open ocean towards Marina
Crossing, the road we had travelled between Medina and
Coral Ridge. Once on the other side, we were officially in the
Centre.

It felt different. The oppressive heavy feeling we had felt
after we left the home of our cousin Ramona was gone. Elva
seemed brighter. She had more colour in her face. "This is
much better!" she said happily.

"What do you mean?" Mannix asked.

"We were here a few weeks ago," Rogue told him. "The
water tasted thick and dirty." She smiled at him. "But that was
when the Destroyer was alive."

He returned her smile, but it was bittersweet. I couldn't
imagine what he was going through. Lady Morgana, the *real*
Lady Morgana, was out there somewhere, dead or alive,
nobody knew. Mannix had been caught in a mental tug of
war for months, knowing the being that bore his love's face
was not her, but a creature that would lay waste to all of
Mattara if given the opportunity. It reminded me of my

parents, back at home, at risk of the worst should they return to Ventura before we could reunite the Heart.

When Ramona saw us, she almost flew to our sides. "What is happening?" she cried. "There is such a change in the waters and I don't understand it!" She clung to her daughter and seemed so grieved; we had to put her out of her misery. She obviously believed something bad had happened. Little did she know that it was something so much bigger than she ever thought possible.

"It's ok, Ramona," I assured her. "Everything's going to be ok now." We told her of our journey and how we came to travel with the Lady… as well as who the Lady turned out to be. Ramona was barely breathing when we finished the story.

"Can it be?" she gasped, eyeing Mannix warily.

"It's true," Mannix nodded. "I killed it myself. The Destroyer is no more." Ramona held her daughter close.

We devoted the following days to trying to find Morgana while we recuperated from the travel and Mannix rested after his bout with the Destroyer. "I don't understand it!" Elva said, frustrated. "I healed you. You should back to perfect health!"

"Your powers just aren't the same here," Rogue told her gently. Elva frowned, unhappy. "It won't last."

"Magic is not a common ability here," Mannix told her. "The naiads have their metamorphosis, but magical born children are rare; very rare, and those that try to learn through study sometimes never gain proficiency."

I rested my hand on Elva's shoulder. "It's possible," I said quietly. "That your powers can only heal physical trauma… and that may not be all Mannix is dealing with." Elva's face changed from anger to pity. She nodded.

With Morgana, Ramona couldn't help us. "I haven't heard of a new girl in the Centre and the Destroyer doesn't really *have* a lair. There are a few towns around that you could check, but I don't believe it will help. If the Destroyer wanted her to disappear, it wouldn't have *hidden* her, it would have… disposed of her," she explained to us.

"I don't believe that," Mannix cut her off. "She's the crown Lady to the heir of Mattara and protected by the Heart of Peace, through her sister. I don't think it even had the power *to* hurt her."

"It's possible she's hidden in one of the towns," Rogue said. "If she's linked to her sister… then she's linked to the Heart," she suggested.

"You think we could find Morgana through Marina?" I asked. "But we were specifically using Morgana to find *Marina?*"

Rogue nodded. "I know. We need one to find the other and right now we can't find either, *but* we might be able to find them through Elva. She's linked to the sister Heart."

Elva nodded. "It could work. I'll try."

We set out the following morning, just as the water began to lighten. We moved to the south, towards Manta Tide, the road between Coral Ridge and Caelios. In the first and second towns, we had no luck. They were small places where everybody knew everybody and there was no sign of any odd behaviour.

The third, Octaria, was the second last village in the area other than the protected village, Inkan, we went through on our arrival in Mattara. Just like the Inkan village, it was a village of cecaelia. Upon seeing the first group of the people, we changed to suit them. Mannix panicked.

"It's ok!" I hissed. "Shh! You'll draw attention!"

The look of alarm remained on his face, but he lowered his spear and stopped yelling, so that was something at least. "How do you do that? That's something the *Destroyer* could do! Changing its appearance at will!"

"That's because we're from the same place," Rogue told him simply, dismounting her seahorse.

We were greeted by shouts and ecstatic screams. A festival was in full swing. It seemed that all of the Centre was rejoicing the expulsion of the evil force that resided within it. We were pulled into the music filled town and without being able to help it, allowed ourselves to be swept up into the celebrations.

"What's going on?" Elva called over the din.

"Can't you feel it?" a cecaelia near us asked, leaping to Elva's side and grabbing her hands. He whirled her around in a dance before sending her off, spinning. "The water is fresh and clear again! We have been celebrating for days!"

"How much longer can they possibly party?" I mumbled, grabbing a hold of Elva before her tentacles could get tangled together. "They have to be near dropping they'd be so tired."

"This is the final night!" the cecaelia announced. "Schools return to their regular classes tomorrow!"

Then the drinks disappeared, the music finally ended and a new day was finally beginning. In the light of day I actually realised there were more triakis and mermaids than I had noticed the previous night. *Maybe it's the tentacles?* Cecaelia did strike such an imposing image it was hard to focus on anything else when there were a lot of them around.

As we looked through the town, we noticed that many of the residents were heading in the same direction. "Where's everybody going?" Elva questioned.

"They must be the students," Mannix told us. "The man last night said that classes start again today."

"Could Morgana be a student?" Rogue asked suddenly, looking around energetically.

"Only one way to find out," I replied. We followed the milling students towards a large building in the western part of town. It was giant slabs of yellow sandstone built into a group of square shapes all linked by long pathways. "Does that remind you of anything?" I asked Rogue.

"Sandcastle," Rogue answered, tilting her head sideways.

"What's a sandcastle?" Mannix asked.

I waved my hand. "Never mind," Rogue answered. "It's a land thing."

"Land?" he repeated, his confusion growing. "Who *are* you people?"

"Later," Elva told him gently. "First, we find Morgana."

Just through the front door, masses of students were opening lockers and reading schedules. "So what kind of school is this?" I asked. "Can't be high school; I'm not sweating… although I *am* underwater…"

"It's a university," Mannix said, pointing. On the wall leading out into an open courtyard was a plaque that read: *Octavia Institute of Science est. 137.*

"Interesting," I said, floating out into the courtyard. Despite being inside a giant sandcastle, the interior courtyard was full of colour. Anemones of every colour lined the pathways and students of every type could be seen lying across giant sea sponges or sitting on the soft grasses, books in front of them, haggard looks on their faces.

"Clearly the students have not recovered from last night," Elva said.

"Definitely not," Rogue agreed, pointing to a triakis off to our left who was staring aimlessly into a small mirror in front of her, pulling at her hair, her eyes bloodshot.

As we gazed around the courtyard, making our way from one side to the other, I noticed a head of blue hair. It was such a pale blue it was almost white and the body was bent over, looking into a book bag. As the cecaelia straightened back up, three of the books fell out.

"Here, let me help," I said as I bent down beside her.

"Thanks," she sighed, finally able to close the bag. As we stood up, she looked up and smiled thankfully.

It was Lady Morgana.

CHAPTER 11

The Lost Lady

§§

"Thanks again," she smiled, before swimming away. I was rooted to the spot. I couldn't move and didn't until Rogue shook me slightly.

"That was Morgana," I said softly, unmoving.

"What?" Mannix frowned, looking around. "Where?"

"That was Morgana…" I repeated slowly. "She's here."

"Where did she go?" he demanded to know.

"Blue hair; almost white, blue hair," I said.

"We search room by room," Rogue said. "Let's go." We scoured the school from top to bottom. Rogue and Elva checked the east wing while Mannix and I searched the west.

"Second row from the front," Mannix whispered to me as we entered the second floor corridor. There she was… We'd actually found her. How was the Destroyer able to keep her here? Why didn't she travel home? Why did no one recognise her? *Why was she a cecaelia?*

As these questions swam around my mind, a distant bell

rang somewhere and we saw the class rise to leave. As they exited into the hallway, both Mannix and me began to tail her, running into Elva and Rogue on the way.

"Hey, we didn't find her!"

"Shh! This way."

"You found her?"

"Which one is she?" I pointed ahead of us to the head of pale blue hair bobbing in and out of view.

We followed her as she left the university, all the way to the other side of town and watched as she disappeared into a building.

"Now what do we do?" Elva asked.

"Wait," Mannix replied quietly. "Morgana never stays home. She is always doing something. After class, she always went riding. It won't be long now. She only has to grab her saddle blanket."

"But we're betting on her sticking to her usual routine," I reminded him. "For all we know, the Destroyer has changed her."

"What are you doing here?" a voice suddenly demanded. We spun around and found another triakis, his tail a reddish hue. He had an oval face, the bottom half of which was covered in a coarse beard. His light brown hair was slicked back to cover the shaved underside. His deep brown eyes were narrowed in suspicion. "Why are you following Olivia?"

"Olivia?" Mannix repeated.

It turned out we didn't need to worry about Morgana not sticking to her routine. At that very moment she came out of her front door, locking it behind her and swam straight over to us. "Hi Rekin, are you ready to go? Who are your friends?"

"Morgana?" Mannix whispered, moving toward her.

"What?" she snapped, confused. "I'm Olivia!"

"They're not friends," the triakis called Rekin told her. "They were following you. I watched them."

"You don't know me?" Mannix asked, shrinking back slightly, ignoring Rekin.

"Should I? What do you want?" she looked at each of us. Upon seeing me, she started slightly. "You helped me with my books this morning!"

"Yes," I nodded. "I'm Ranger. Olivia, is it?" I asked her. "Yes?"

"We have a message for someone who fits your description," Rogue told her. "But you don't seem recognise Mannix. If you were who we were looking for, you would."

"I'm Olivia," she repeated, folding her arms. "Who are you looking for exactly?"

I turned to Rogue, unsure. Morgana didn't know who she was anymore. What were we supposed to say? "We're looking for the Lady Morgana," Elva told her. I shot her a look, but she just shrugged. "The truth hasn't led me astray before."

Her frown changed to a look of confusion. "Lady *Morgana?* What are you talking about?" Rekin laughed.

Not-Morgana joined him. "How do I look *anything* like the Lady?"

"You're a spitting image to us," Elva said softly.

"You're crazy!" She turned her back to us and swam swiftly away, not looking back.

Rekin followed. "You have the wrong person," he said as he left.

We were left alone, at a loss of what to do. The Destroyer had found the best way of getting rid of someone. It had hidden her in the one place she couldn't be rescued from… her own mind.

It wasn't until Mannix spoke that we snapped out of our trance. "She doesn't know who she is…" he whispered softly. "And who is *Rekin?*"

"We need to jog her memory," Rogue said. "How?"

I looked to the others and at the ground. I thought for a moment before looking up once more. "Elva," I whispered.

"Me? What can I do?"

"Show her the truth," I answered, pulling a photo out of Mannix's pack and a small hand held mirror out of Rogue's.

Armed with the mirror and photo, we waited out the front of her building for her to return. When she did, she was alone, Rekin nowhere in sight. Before the door could close, we slipped in after her. She turned around at the lack of sound from the door closing.

"What are you doing here?" she yelled. "GET OUT!"

"No, Morgana," Rogue said hardly. "You need to listen to us. Pleas~?"

"~MY NAME IS OLIVIA!" she screeched. "Not Morgana! You people are crazy!"

"Oh really?" I asked. I concentrated on the mermaids passing by outside and watched as the eight tentacles streaming from my hips became one. Morgana looked horrified.

"Who are you people?" she gasped, moving backwards.

"What is your story of Rogue and Ranger?" Elva asked.

"What has *that* got to do with anything?"

"Centuries ago a Heart was left to a Guardian here in Mattara. The present day Guardian is Lady Marina, sister to Lady Morgana. Morgana was taken and replaced by the Destroyer so it could get closer to the Guardian. It hid the real Morgana," I said.

Not~Olivia was shaking her head in disbelief. Elva took the mirror from Mannix and gave it to Morgana. She slowly reached for it. "The Destroyer wiped your memory and placed a fake one in its stead," Elva told her. "He altered your appearance so no one else would recognise you, including yourself… but I am the Guardian of the Heart of Truth and I am able to see it wherever it lies. You are the Lady and we will prove it to you."

Mannix gave her the photo and after looking at it, she turned to him. "This is you… and the Lady," she whispered.

"It is *us*," he corrected her. "On our anniversary last year. Your parents… the Lord and Lady, took this photo. Up until the Destroyer replaced you in the palace and had me banned from it, it was hanging on a wall in your bedroom… It was the only thing I was able to bring with me."

"Look into the mirror," Elva instructed her. "Let it show you the truth. A mirror cannot lie." Standing behind her as Morgana looked into the mirror, the magic of the pink Heart of Valeria washed over her.

Before she could respond the door burst open and Rekin came charging in, a double bladed axe in his hands. "GET AWAY FROM HER!" he roared. He froze when he saw the pink glow engulf Morgana. "*What did you do?*"

Her eyes wavered slightly before she blinked. Morgana gasped and dropped the mirror, which was less dramatic than it sounds given we were underwater. She cried out, doubling over. Her tentacles melted together and became a royal blue tail with three fins on either side. Her hair exploded with colour, turning a bright aqua blue and her eyes iced over.

Mannix fell to her side and held her as she sobbed. She shook slightly at his touch, but soon she had her arms wrapped around his broad shoulders and he was squeezing her tightly as though he'd never let go.

Rekin let his axe fall to his side, stunned. "Olivia?"

Mannix and Morgana very slowly got back up. Morgana wiped her face and sniffed a few times. "Rekin. Thank you for everything you did for me. You have been a loyal and trustworthy friend," she told him. "My name is Morgana." He continued to stare, shaking his head, struggling to understand what was happening. "The Destroyer tried to force me to disclose my sister's location. When I refused I found myself trapped. I was seeing through my eyes, but I couldn't control my body. The words coming out of my mouth weren't mine. I was… Olivia."

"You *are* the Lady Morgana?"

Morgana smiled gently before turning to us and exhaling deeply. "Thank you, Elva," she shuddered slightly. "You'll never know just what this means to me. You've given me my life back."

"Well, we weren't going to let a little something like avoiding kidnapping someone get in the way of finding you, now were we?" I joked. Rogue gave me a pained look. "Right, not the time."

Morgana laughed; a light, melodious sound. She turned to Mannix, holding his head in her hands. "You knew… You always knew."

"Of course I knew," he said to her, kissing her hands. "Nothing was going to stop me from finding you."

She smiled and embraced him again, before pulling away and turning to Rekin. He remained in the doorway, too nervous to move, too curious to leave. "Rekin, will you join us?"

"Join you?"

"The journey to my sister is dangerous," she said. "We'll need all the help me can get." Rekin nodded resolutely. Morgana nodded back, smiling. "I'll take you to my sister. She's very anxious to see you," she told us, sighing. "And me."

CHAPTER 12

Chasms & Conspiracies

§§

"Are we there yet?" Elva complained. "I need a break."

"Do *not* start that," Rogue growled unhappily as she bounced around in the saddle.

From Octaria we had follow Manta Tide back to Coral Ridge, then headed north along Chasm Road. It had meant a lot of time in the saddle. I knew that Elva was not trying to be difficult. She couldn't withstand this world for much longer. From the time we'd found Morgana she had started to feel sluggish and slow. The Destroyer being gone had helped, but only for so long. She was deteriorating again. We needed to find a way home as soon as possible *and* get the note that Raven had left for us. Would the paper not disintegrate underwater?

"It isn't much farther," Morgana replied. "We are going to the Chasm."

Fear shot through my body and made my tail tingle, which

was the strangest sensation I'd experienced thus far. "I'm sorry, is this not the same Chasm that holds Mattara's largest shellfish? The ones that devour all that venture too close to the edge?"

"That is the Great Chasm," Morgana explained. "Where we are going is a much smaller Chasm that runs off of it. It is there my sister waits for us."

"Are there shellfish in this one too?" Elva asked faintly.

"Of course... except they're much smaller," Rekin answered, turning to her.

"That's comforting," Rogue frowned. "And the feral naiads?"

"The *what?*" Rekin said.

"Morgana sa-oh!" I stopped short. "That was a lie!"

"What was a lie?" Morgana asked curiously.

"The Destroyer said the naiads often remove themselves from greater society and stay secluded in the Chasm for the peace and quiet, but it leads them to... *revert?* I guess? It said they become vicious and attack people who get too close."

"Well, to be fair, most anyone will attack something or someone that threatens their home," Rekin pointed out. "But no, the naiads of the Chasm remain of perfectly sound mind. They *can* be dangerous, but only because they are weary of the dangers that surround them and they *did* specifically move there to be away from people. They definitely don't welcome visitors."

"Either way, they'll have no reason to bother us," Morgana assured us. "They tend to keep to themselves. We'll see them, but they will be far more interested in seeing us get taken by the shellfish."

We continued, moving towards the large gaping hole in the ground ahead of us. *Since we're in water, it's not as if we can fall off the edge, so I guess that's a good thing...*

As we neared the edge, Elva lurched forward on her seahorse and almost fell off. "What is it?" I asked her anxiously as she clutched the locket around her neck.

"I feel it!" she gasped. "The Heart. It feels like..." she drifted off into a whisper and closed her eyes. "Home." The closer we got to the Chasm, the more colour seemed to appear in her face.

"We leave the seahorses here," Morgana instructed, pointing to posts stuck deep into the ground. "They can go back with the next tour bus."

I tied Night Light to the post and thanked him for what he and the others had done for us. Being seahorses, I highly doubted they understood what my meaning was, but they'd taken care of us and deserved recognition.

I returned to the edge with Mannix and joined Morgana, Rekin, Rogue and Elva. "Where do we find her?" Rogue asked.

Morgana pointed into the depths of the Chasm, right in the middle. "At the very bottom."

We floated over the threshold and into open water, letting

ourselves be propelled downward, with the weight of the water. I could hear Rogue breathing heavily next to me. I reached out and grasped her hand. This was no different to any other heights experience for her.

Long after our ears popped, I began to notice small fissures in the rock. I was about to ask about them when I noticed tiny tentacles protruding out of them. A shiver ran down my spine and a small squeak escaped my lips. Not far away, in the Great Chasm, were gigantic versions of those tiny creatures; where their little shells were no bigger than eyeballs to their larger counterparts. I shivered again.

As we got further down, the water grew colder. It wasn't long before we were all shivering. The water was also becoming turbulent, like we had been trapped in a riptide. There was a pulling feeling that came in short bursts. We were quickly sucked down with each one.

"It's all right!" Morgana called out to us over the sound of the rushing water. "It's just for security!"

I started to calm down. It was normal. It was fine… then I saw what was causing it. It was a giant mouth; a huge, gaping hole at the bottom of the Chasm, teeth and all, taking huge, sweeping breaths in.

Elva screamed, turned on her tail and began clawing her way upwards. Rogue and I were extremely close to following her. "STOP HER!" Mannix roared. "GET HER BACK!"

I grabbed at her, but she was out of my reach. As I was

slowly pulled away from her, there was a yell from behind me and Rekin leapt forward, wrapping his arms around her middle. She froze up, her hand flying to her neck, the necklace pulsing brightly.

The second she froze, Rogue threw herself at the both of them, just as the gaping maw opened and breathed in again, dragging us all, screaming, right into the colossal creature's mouth.

Elva was still screaming when we opened our eyes on the other side. Her voice slowly drifted away as she realised what was happening. We had not been eaten by the creature. We were not in a stomach. We were in a vast cave, overladen with shells, starfish and seaweed. Rogue released Rekin, who released Elva in turn, who continued to breathe as though she had run a race. "Will you be alright?" Rekin asked her, his hands up in front of him protectively.

Elva nodded rapidly in short, jerky motions. "Yes," she puffed, holding the necklace in her hand. "Yes, I will be fine." As the necklace started glowing brighter, the pulsing light became faster and Elva began to calm. "She's close," she whispered. "Or the Heart is, at least."

"She is here," Morgana confirmed, eyes closed. "She is waiting for us." We followed the steady beating of the Valerian Heart. From its place around Elva's neck, the pale pink glow grew stronger, getting brighter and brighter with every beat.

Elva's breathing had become regular again, evening out, but she swam faster. We followed, faster and faster, until the pull of Elva's sister Heart had us speeding through the caverns so quickly that had someone been watching us, we would have been no more than colourful blurs.

"*Marina!*" we heard Morgana cry out. We stopped short at a large archway in the cavern wall. From it drifted long tendrils of seaweed and kelp, creating a thick curtain blocking our view. The Lady and Guardian Marina was only on the other side and the Mattaran Heart of Peace lay with her... and once we had them both, Morgana would once again be left with only Mannix, unable to see her sister. I glanced at Rekin beside me. He stared straight at the seaweed curtain, regarding it with caution.

"Are you ready?" Elva asked Morgana, placing a hand on her shoulder.

"No, I'm not," she replied, breathless. "I spent so long as Olivia, thinking I was going crazy because I was hearing someone's voice inside my head... never knowing that all along... it was my sister. Now I'm finally going to see her again, only to lose her. I won't be alright for quite some time."

We all fell silent as Rekin slowly drew back the seaweed veil. One by one, we followed Morgana and Mannix through the slimy plant and into the cave beyond.

Once again, we meet...

Romira?

Yes, it is I.

You know us from Valeria?

No, I am different from the Heart of Valeria, worn by the young elven fairy you arrive with. While I have never met this young woman, I am connected to her through the sister Heart she wears.

You're not the same person within each Heart?

I am the same soul, but the essence of each Heart has changed. I am the Heart of Peace; therefore I am different to the Heart Miss Elva carries, the Heart of Truth. Though the Hearts still remain Romira... we cannot help but be impacted by the Guardians we share our existence with.

You know Elva?

I know her being, through the connection of the Hearts. You are very near your goal. The Guardian awaits you. I can feel she longs for her sister. She is in much distress. You would do well to give her time with her before you enter. I believe it will lead you to what you seek.

Romira?

Yes Ranger?

Are you happy being separate from your body, unable to move on?

I will be able to move on someday... when my work is done and Ventura is safe. Until that day comes, however, Marina guards me well. Many a stray fisherfolk have been lost to her wrath. It is odd. She is a fierce Guardian, but she is not as attuned to me as expected.

How do you mean?

Elva and I are one, I can feel it. She is completely connected to the Heart of Truth. It is not the same with Marina and I.

What does that mean? I didn't know how a connection to a Guardian in Valeria would be any different to one here in Mattara.

I felt a great deal closer to my last Guardian. It is strange. I still feel that connection at times.

How is that possible?

You should speak to your triakis friend… He knows… Romira's voice started to fade.

Who? Mannix?

No…

Romira's voice slowly faded away, but the dim blue light at the end of the cave grew steadily brighter, leading us towards Marina. We slowed down; letting Morgana get so far ahead of us we lost sight of her.

"We need to go faster," Mannix urged, speeding up.

"No," Rekin whispered. "Let her go." Mannix frowned at him, unhappy at being questioned. "She needs to do this alone."

Long minutes trickled slowly by as we crept along at a snail's pace. I surveyed Rekin suspiciously. Romira said he knew something about the connection with the Heart. I decided to find out what. "How did you come to meet Morgana?" I asked him. "When she was Olivia, I mean?"

He looked surprised by the question. "We… we went to school together," he answered, like it was obvious. "Met in the courtyard one morning when the university was running riding trials for the school's competing team. Why?"

"You just seem very protective of her, that's all, and you can't have known her long. I thought maybe you had feelings for her."

At this, Rekin chuckled. "No, our friendship was not like that at all. She's a Lady of Mattara. She needed protection." He paused, realising he had given himself away.

"*You knew?*" I hissed as loudly as I dared, dropping back from the others. "Who *are* you?"

He paled, which was hard given how pale he already was. He looked to the others, then back to me, reaching to his belt. I clenched my fist, my hand glowing deep green. "*Don't.*"

"I won't if you won't," he replied, raising his hands.

I let the glow die down, but it didn't disappear entirely. "Talk," I ordered.

"I was sent to protect her."

"*Sent?* By who?"

"By Romira." At this I stopped entirely. He turned back to me, nodding. "Yes, that's right. Romira told me Morgana was in Octaria under the control of the Destroyer. I was to keep her safe until the Destroyer was eliminated, or Morgana regained her memories.”

“How?” I asked flatly. “What is your connection to the Heart?”

Rekin’s body seemed to droop in the water. “I was apprenticed to the last Guardian,” he said finally, pain in his eyes. “I could always feel Romira, but it wasn’t until the Guardian died that he started *talking* to me.” He shook his head, looking down and rubbing his eyes.

“The Guardian has *apprentices?*”

Rekin nodded. “Not for Guardianship. The Guardian was a carver; a master craftsman. He was teaching me.”

“So… you were around the Heart a lot?”

“From my earliest days. When it started talking to me it was… a *buzzing*, at first; too jumbled to make out, but when his voice finally came through, he told me to find Morgana in Octaria, that she wouldn’t know who she was and no one would recognise her.”

“But you did?”

He shook his head again. “I don’t know why, but yes. I recognised her the moment I saw her. She looked the same to me. I don’t know what anyone else saw when they looked at her, but she was only ever Morgana to me.”

“So you planted yourself into her life,” I finished for him, continuing on through the cave. The others had reached an open clam shell door; the entrance to an inner chamber. Rogue looked back at me questioningly. I waved her on and they passed through the door. "Did Romira talk to you again?"

"Every now and again the buzz will return, but nothing definitive."

"Not even now?"

"No? Why?"

"He spoke to me," I answered. "When we first entered the cavern."

"What did he say?" Rekin asked earnestly. We approached the clam shell door, which still lay open.

"That his connection with Marina isn't the same as it was with your mentor," I answered. "He can't figure out why, but the powers of the Heart of Peace are impacted by it. He seemed to imply that Marina was only able to physically protect him, but not magically using the Heart." We edged our way through the door, and found the sisters enveloped around each other, Morgana's cries echoing around the cavern. At the sound of our arrival, Marina looked up and her eyes narrowed.

"What happened to her?" she hissed at Mannix.

Her appearance shocked us. As twins, of course she looked like Morgana; but there was a wild look about her that electrified the air. Her hair was shock white and her fingernails were long, curved talons. She wore a headdress of what appeared to be fish scales and she held in her hand a shell and pearl sceptre. Her tail was a lime colour, matching the soft green of her eyes and scales like those on her headdress covered her chest like armour. Her skin was tanned, despite not seeing any light, but her anger had sent her cheeks burning red.

"She hasn't been herself for quite some time," Elva was trying to explain.

"I can see that," Marina snapped. "Mannix; why did you not protect her?"

"Protect her? The Destroyer took her at a time when I was not with her!" Mannix exploded. "It had me run out of the palace before I could do anything about it! I spent *weeks* tracking it down and I *killed it!* EVEN THOUGH IT HAD HER FACE!" His voice broke. "What more could you have asked of me?"

The fire in Marina's face did not die as she let her sister go and drew herself up to her full height. Her eyebrow raised, she looked us up and down. Then she struck the ground with her staff, causing another large shell door to open to her left. "Follow me," she ordered, taking her sister's hand and leading us all into the room beyond.

CHAPTER 13
Stirring

§§

"Havoc is coming… Havoc is coming… Havoc is coming!" Ariannah continued to mutter and mumble in her sleep as Ford took yet another watch over her. This had been occurring for weeks now, with Ariannah never being left without an official keeping watch. Since the meeting when Queen Eleria informed the other Advisors to the Crown, Ariannah had a troop of twelve guards, three selected by each advisor, and the four city officials of the Observatory took shifts to ensure one of them was always there, ready to inform Eleria and the other Advisors should the situation change.

Ariannah had begun to talk in her sleep. What had begun as mumbling and groaning, had turned into her repeating the same sentence over and over. Once it started, it would last a few hours, then she would fall back into her deep sleep.

Ariannah had slept soundly for almost two weeks, when all of sudden, she had begun her repetition again and had continued with increasing vigour. Whatever was happening in her mind, it was clearly causing her distress.

"Sir!" a voice cut into Ford's thoughts, bringing him to attention.

"Yes?"

"The Queen has arrived, Sir," a sprite informed him. "She in en route."

"Thank you, Jetta. Return to your quarters." Jetta the sprite nodded and left.

Eleria arrived within minutes. "What has happened."

"She has begun again," Ford informed her. "It started six hours ago; always the same thing."

"Havoc is coming… Havoc is coming… Havoc is coming…"

"What is going *on?*" Eleria asked helplessly as she watched Ariannah sleeping in her crystal case.

♠

On the shores of Lake Viridian, just outside the Port Nixin city boundary, Prince Fallon and Fillipe were welcoming the final group of students to the newly named Champion Sporting Academy of Health and Fitness. A grand total of twelve dormitories had been built to house the almost two hundred orphaned students who had requested to attend.

Now the testing was to begin. Each student had a number of streams to choose from and rigorous challenges to complete in order to evaluate their current skill level. This would determine how their schooling would continue from that point forward.

Coaches and trainers had been shipped in from all over Valeria to cover every possible sporting ability. Health and medical educators were also brought in for the students that were there to study the body and its functions in sporting prowess, including the development of healing protocols that directly related to sporting injuries.

Here was where the students could show the coaches what skills they had. They would follow two streams of education; one skill based and another interest based. This maximised the student's potential to build on what they were good at, as well as further explore and develop skills in their passions.

Fillipe was incredibly excited about the next stage of the school. With the orphaned kids of Valeria all finding places where they belonged and felt wanted and accepted, came the potential for a new age of progress. These students would grow into adults with all the skills and drive to succeed and give them the best possible start to adult life. The time of orphans aging out of the system with no support and no ability to thrive as successful adults was coming to an end, and it would be because of the schools he and Fallon had seen to fruition.

The Champion Sporting Academy doubled down on this

task, because not only was it housing the greatest number of students of all the new schools, but a great number of its tutors, coaches and trainers had been found on the streets of Valeria's cities. The large number of orphans that aged out of the system only to find there was nowhere for them to go ended up homeless, and those that did not have marketable skills often stayed that way. These orphans, as it so happened, were also often physically skilled, making them prime candidates for roles at the Academy.

Prince Fallon had begun the tour for the students, taking them through the dormitories. Fillipe turned back to his group, thirty four youths in their late teens and early twenties, with weary, gaunt looks on their faces. Many had fought the idea of working at the Academy, fearing it was a trick, but as word had gotten around Valeria, more and more people wanted to be involved, and Fillipe and Prince Fallon were committed to finding a place for every single one of them.

♠

In Eliad, a ship had been docked for almost two months. The hooded stranger who had stolen aboard after its docking in Port Nixin had long since made his way off the ship. He had immediately found a stable and stolen a horse, which had sped his way to the Capitol.

Upon his arrival, he was stopped by guards. "State your

business!" the fairy guard, Fabian, barked.

"I'm here to see Queen Eleria," the stranger announced, a silver dagger strapped to his waist.

The Queen however, remained safe and sound at the Observatory, which was under strict lockdown. No one was allowed in and no one was allowed out. Evanna, Glenrock and Naevia had joined Ford and Eleria in Ariannah's medical chamber, deep in the foundations of the Observatory.

"We can't possibly let this go on!" Evanna was saying.

"We don't know why this is happening," Queen Eleria replied. "There's no reason to make any formal decisions unless we have cause."

"If she wakes, she could destroy us all!" Glenrock growled. "We should remove the risk immediately!"

"What does Elva have to say about this?" Naevia's Observatory official, Deacon, asked.

"She was adamant that she was the only one that could wake Ariannah and I trust her," Eleria said, looking meaningfully at Ford and Evanna.

"Should she not come and see for herself?" Xenos, the fairy official asked.

"We would not risk bringing her here, or indeed, anywhere out in the open, if it wasn't absolutely necessary," Eleria answered. "Evanna, Glenrock, Naevia; we make this decision together. Do you think Ariannah merely stirring in her sleep warrants placing our Guardian at risk?"

Evanna crumpled in her husband's arms. Glenrock's shoulders dropped and Naevia's light dulled. They each shook their heads silently.

Eleria nodded. "We watch… and we wait."

Lying in the crystal case in front of the city officials and Advisors to the Crown, Ariannah continued to shift in her sleep, as her dreams continued.

The man is back in the room, surrounded by the mirrors. His breath is coming heavier. His chest is aching, like his heart is breaking… but he has to continue. One last visit to each; that is all he has left in him.

The mirrors on the walls all around him are shifting and warping, distorting their reflected images. As he looks into the one in front of him, he cannot even recognise the face looking back at him as his own.

He gets to his feet and makes his way to the closest mirror. He can smell a light fragrance wafting out, and as he allows himself to fall forward, he hears a long, low howl begin, far off in the distance.

CHAPTER 14
Pomp & Uncontrollable Circumstance

§§

Taking a seat in a mother of pearl throne and gesturing for her sister to sit on a squishy sea sponge beside her, the Lady and Guardian Marina, signed for us to come closer.

"I know who you are and what it is that you want," she began.

"Marina~," Mannix started.

She raised her hand, commanding him into silence. "You sought me out looking for the Mattaran Heart of Peace. With you, you brought the elven fairy from a distant world, linked to our own through the Hearts we both bear.

"Unknowingly, you brought with you the Destroyer, who you claim was killed by Mannix here; a feat that no other has ever come close to. You learned of my sister's existence in the Centre and freed her from the prison within her mind.

"Morgana brought you to me, knowing full well the consequences of doing such a thing. Being who you are, I had no choice, not only to forgive her behaviour, and allow you into my domain when I would otherwise have disposed of you." There, she paused for a moment to take off her headdress, allowing a head of white blonde hair to fall halfway down her back.

"The Destroyer is dead, Mannix's name has been cleared and my sister is free… All this has happened due to your arrival," Marina continued with a gracious bravado. "It is because of this that I have decided to join you. Just as this…" she gestured towards us. "*Elva,* has accompanied you, so will I. It is my duty as Guardian of the Heart of Mattara to make sure that the magic that protects this world doesn't fail."

How did she know who we were? Who Elva was? What we were doing? And how did she know that we needed her? "The Heart's reach encompasses *all* of Mattara. Every movement, every whisper… everything comes to me in time," she told us. It was as though she'd read our thoughts.

At this point Rogue began wandering around the room, touching and looking at all the shells placed in it. I eyed her off, looking from her to Marina, to gauge her reaction at the perceived disrespect. Marina's eyes followed her with an almost dangerous deliberation.

Rogue continued her exploration, either oblivious or uncaring of Marina's critical eye. Some of the shells were as large as a young whale. Others were so small they could only hold grains of sand. It was one of the medium sized clam shells that hung around Marina's neck, pulsing a bright, aqua blue.

"Can we see your Heart?" Elva asked suddenly, moving towards Marina.

After a few moments of silent consideration, Marina came forward and opened the clam shell. Inside was an intricately woven, silver charm in the shape of a fish tail, the blue shine glowing from its centre.

"I've spent many years of my life protecting the Heart, and by doing so, protecting my entire world," Marina told us. "I hope you understand the risk I'm taking by leaving this world with it."

"You are not the only Guardian who will have to," Elva reminded her. "Or have you already forgotten how I came to be here? All of us will have to take a risk or *all* the worlds of Ventura will be destroyed. Instead of letting the *Lady* in you go to your head, remember that you are a *Guardian!*"

Marina seemed to have been struck dumb, regarding her curiously. It was like she was unsure of whether or not to get angry. Morgana came forward. "Marina… it's just us here," she said softly. "No Ladies, just sisters… Don't let Mother and Father's expectations control how you behave. You're a Guardian. You can be better than this… You *are* better than this!" she pleaded.

Marina held Morgana's gaze for a long time, as though some private, silent exchange was occurring. She finally sighed, dropping her shoulders and sitting back down on her throne. "You are right Morgana. I am, first and foremost, the Guardian." She let go of the staff and headdress, which was still on her lap and let them drift to the floor of the cave. "When you've been raised to behave and see yourself in a very specific way, it can be a rather difficult habit to break.

"You are right, Elva. It is my duty to protect the Heart and make sure it is united with its sisters… whatever that means for me." Marina got up once more. "We have to return to the palace. Our parents need to know of the Destroyer's death, Morgana's possession and Mannix's innocence. There are also some goodbyes that obviously need to be said… and I'd rather say them at home."

"There's some unfinished business we have also," Rogue told her.

"Ramona?" I questioned under my breath. Rogue nodded.

"Alright then," Marina reached down and lifted the pearl and shell sceptre. It was omitting a pulsing blue glow to match the Heart around Marina's neck. The blue glow overcame us all and when the light retracted back into the sceptre, we were in the entrance hall of Coral Palace.

The sound of a hundred gasps ran through the crowd before an awed silence captured them all. "Good afternoon people of Medina!" Marina called to them. "The Coral Palace will be receiving no visitors for the rest of the day; I need to debrief my parents! Please return in the morning!" Within moments, the entire crowd had vanished out the doors and the great hall entrance was clear. With Morgana and Marina in the lead, we entered the hall and were greeted by the cries of their long-missed parents.

We stayed back, allowing the family time for their reunification, but they soon pulled us over. "You will never understand how much this means to us," Oceana told us, speaking for her and Morgan. "You brought both our daughters home, cleared Mannix's name and destroyed the Destroyer!"

"Our World is at peace at last! Oh, how Mattara will rejoice! We will go down in *history* as the Lord and Lady of the Golden Age!"

"What is your name, son? Rekin?"

"Oh, he'll have to be knighted of *course!*"

"It was Mannix who defeated the Destroyer, not us. That shows you the devotion he has to Morgana. Let us hope that this miscommunication never happens again," Rogue said flatly, disinterested in their flattery.

"What are we doing here, stuffed in a corner?" Lord Morgan cried out, either ignoring or completely missing her rudeness. "Tonight a party, tomorrow a wedding!"

♠

The next afternoon, we were assembled in the gardens of South-East Point; Mannix's hometown. It was where he and Morgana had always planned to get married and begin their life in their own home. Hundreds of people filled the gardens, if not thousands. It seemed like everyone in the city had made a point of attending, as well as every Aristocratic family from Medina and half of Mattara besides. Clearly anybody who felt like they were *anybody* was going to be there for the wedding of Lady Morgana and the soon to be Lord Mannix, *saviour* of Mattara and destroyer of the Destroyer.

Mannix had been taken aback by how the people had begun to refer to him, blushing fiercely. "That sounds ridiculous. *Destroyer of the Destroyer?*" He was standing in front of the mirror at his parents' house, struggling with his bow tie. "What kind of hair-brained ninny came up with th– WHY DOESN'T THIS THING WORK?"

Rekin chuckled and went to tie his bow tie for him. "Let me."

"Thank you," Mannix sighed.

Morgana looked beautiful surrounded by all of the corals and sea flowers in bloom. Her dress looked amazing, though strange due to the underwater effect on the material. Rekin and Marina stood by her side, the only real friends she'd ever had, while Mannix was flanked by his two younger brothers.

After the ceremony, the bride and groom were whisked

away to open presents and have their first dance as man and wife. Whilst that was happening, Rogue, Elva, Marina and me were escorted to Mannix's house by his cousin, Monty.

"I gave this box to Mannix myself, the day I became Guardian twelve years ago. I told him that it was vital this box be lodged in South-East Point," Marina told us, pulling the box off a shelf in the kitchen. "It's never been opened by anyone other than me." She opened the box and reached inside, pulling out a still white envelope.

So here it was; the letter that had long awaited us from Raven. It was Rogue who opened it and read the letter out loud to us.

♠

Rogue and Ranger

By coming this far, you have done well. The Guardians of Mattara are the only eyes to have seen these writings, though its knowledge is meant for you.

In the world of Valeria, there was a city called North-East Point and here in Mattara, there is a South-East Point. You will also find a South-West Point and a North-West Point. These four cities are points that link the entire map of Ventura Estate and therefore, the Venturan worlds. These cities link the worlds more closely than you know.

If you found my last letter, you will also have received the glass case in which the Heart of Ventura was kept. Only when the Heart is completely restored, can it be placed in the case.

I leave with you now something worth more to the family of Ventura than life itself; a book never before opened. Only a Royce can read its pages. Had Raphael gotten his hands on it, the fate of the Venturan worlds would have long been decided. It holds all the information needed to defeat him. I wish you all the luck.

Raven

"It's been written on cloth with waterproof ink," I said in awe. "Raven was obviously very smart...."

"Where is the book?" Elva asked suddenly. Marina turned to us, her eyes grave.

"What is it?" I questioned, my heart sinking.

"The day I became Guardian, the Coral Palace was broken into-" she began.

"-WHAT DO YOU MEAN 'BROKEN INTO'?" Rogue exploded.

"The book was stolen... by the Destroyer... Nobody knows what happened to it," she said, holding her head down in shame.

"If the book was to remain in South-East Point, why was

it moved when you became Guardian?"

"It's customary for it to be with the Guardian for that first day before being returned to South-East Point," she explained to us.

"So now that the Destroyer is dead, how do we find it?" Elva whispered softly.

"We already know where it is and who has it!" I insisted. "The second the Destroyer had access to that book, he made sure he was able to steal it… so he could give it to Raphael!"

"The book in the glass cabinet!" Rogue gasped. "It was there the whole time… Raphael has the book!"

"The Destroyer couldn't have given it directly to Raphael; he's a spirit," I began. "The only thing it could do is send it through the mirror back to the castle and hope Raphael got it first."

"But it was in the glass case with the box that had the deed in it," Rogue went on.

"The book is in a glass case?" Elva asked suddenly.

"Yeah, with the deed."

"Then Raphael couldn't have it," she said, smiling.

"What do you mean?"

"Spirits can't move through glass," Elva announced, her face flushing with excitement. "At least not in Valeria…but it would also explain why he was never able to get the deed either!" I could have kissed her. She stood there, crossing her arms, a smug smile on her face.

"Um… excuse me?" Marina asked delicately. "Who's Raphael?" We all turned to look at her, various looks of shock and indignation on our faces. She looked uncomfortable. "What?"

CHAPTER 15

Once is a Coincidence... Twice is a Pattern

§§

We all stared at her, dumbstruck. "You don't know who Raphael is?"

"Raven's husband~?"

"~Tried to take over the worlds~?"

"~Raven gave the Heart to Mattara to *protect it from him?*" Marina shook her head, confusion on her face. "*None* of this is familiar?"

Marina shook her head again. "That's not possible!" Elva exclaimed, moving forward to look Marina in the eye.

"What?" Marina repeated again, getting defensive. "Who is Raphael? What does he have to do with any of this?"

"Marina," Rogue began. "Raphael is the reason for *all* of this. He is why you're a Guardian at all."

"Raven brought the Heart of Romira to Mattara centuries ago," I told her. "She was hiding it from her husband,

Raphael. He was trying to use to take over the worlds of Ventura. Raven thought if she hid pieces of the Heart in each world then Raphael wouldn't be able to get into them and the worlds could then use the pieces to protect themselves."

"What do you mean by 'pieces'?"

Elva was holding her face. She looked terrified. "How could you be bonded to a Heart and not know this?" she exclaimed. "The pieces of the Heart were each given to a Guardian; *seven* in total. You have the Heart of Peace; I have the Heart of Truth, both traits Romira highly valued."

"There are *seven worlds?*" Marina gasped. "I knew about the land world… and there are times I get glimpses of another… I think. I knew the gravest of errors had occurred when the book was stolen but I never knew so much of Mattara's history and knowledge of the Heart and its origins had been lost to me!" She turned away in distress. "I thought that surely Liang would inform me of what I needed to know!"

"NO!" Elva cried in panic. "Romira should have! That's what being bonded to a Heart *is!* It is a deep unwavering connection to the very essence of Romira's being!"

"Well then, I guess I don't have it, do I?" Marina finally snapped, her face red with embarrassment. "I've done my best to be the Guardian Mattara needed and deserved, but despite choosing me, I've *never* been able to use the Heart the way Liang or the other Guardians that came before me could!

My parents thought it was because Liang was still alive, but even after he was killed *nothing changed!*" Both she and Elva seemed devastated at the revelation.

"The Destroyer... when it was Morgana, said that your parents wanted Liang to stay at the palace, but they refused... then they were dead within a year," I remembered. "Did your parents have the old Guardian killed in an attempt to boost your power?"

Marina looked at us, her face contorted in pain. "How we are perceived by the people of Mattara is everything to my parents. Our image is what they spend every day of their lives cultivating," she said softly, choking back a sob. "I don't know if they ordered the attack on Liang; I was already hidden in the Chasm... but if I were to learn they had, it would not come as a shock."

"Wait," Elva interrupted. "Liang was *alive* when he passed on the Guardianship, but it glowed for Marina anyway," she said, pacing the room. "This would definitely account for the damage or disconnect in the link to the Heart. A new Guardian can't possibly connect with Romira properly while a prior connection remains intact."

"Yes," I nodded. "But Liang *died*."

"Says who? The Destroyer? Oceana and Morgan? The only real information we have is the Heart. What does *it* say?"

"Romira spoke to me in the Chasm," I announced. "He said that his connection with Marina was not the same as the others, but he couldn't understand why."

"What else did he say?" Rogue asked.

"That Rekin did." I proceeded to tell them what I'd learned about Rekin and his apprenticeship to Liang.

"You kept this from us?" Rogue asked angrily.

"Not on purpose!" I said. "We met Marina and went back to the palace and then I forgot because it just didn't seem important until now!"

"You're saying you think that Rekin's exposure to the Heart from his apprenticeship has altered the Heart's ability to connect with Marina?" Elva asked.

"He *did* say that Romira started talking to him only after Liang died."

"So does Liang live or not?" Marina asked desperately.

"If Liang is alive… Rekin knows," I answered, heading for the door.

The wedding reception was still in full swing. People around us danced. The twelve tier cake was almost half gone and guests appeared dazed and sloppy having partied for as long as they had.

Sitting at the head table was Oceana, Morgana and an older mermaid they hadn't seen before. "Aunt Moira," Marina greeted. "How are y-?"

"~AND *HERE'S* OUR GUARDIAN!" Aunt Moira screeched. "Oh, how I tell your stories my dear! My friends *love* hearing all about your adventures!"

"I stay in my cave and guard the Heart, Aunt Moira. I don't *have* adventures," she responded flatly.

"*Mind your aunt, Marina!*" Lady Oceana hissed angrily, before planting a giant fake smile on her face. "Oh, you need to hear the story of how Mannix killed the Destroyer! They'll be talking about it for *centuries!*"

As the mermaids began to babble away, Marina gave a pitying smile to Morgana, who mirrored it in return. "Where's Rekin?"

"He went looking for Mannix," Morgana answered with a sigh. "He said he had to collect something from his house and he'd be right back, but that was an hour ago, so I asked Rekin to see where he'd gotten to. Is everything ok?" She looked worried.

We exchanged nervous glances. "Morgana… we were just there," I told her. "Mannix hasn't been there at all."

"What are you saying?" Morgana stood up and swam over the table. "Mannix is gone?"

"And so is Rekin," Rogue groaned.

"We have to find them," Marina told her sister. Morgana nodded, and together, we began the search. We headed to the entrance to the gardens and asked the members of security, but no one had seen Mannix or Rekin. "Thank you gentlemen."

Outside the gardens, twinkling lights in the form of glowing sea urchins lit the streets, but all was calm and quiet. "Let's circle around the edge of the gardens and work our way in," Morgana suggested. "The gardens are huge. It's possible they just went to get some peace and quiet from the party. Neither of them appreciate crowds very much, and you know Mannix; he can't stand being fussed over. Aunt Moira *alone* was enough for him for a lifetime!"

Marina, Morgana and Elva went in one direction and Rogue and I went in the other, making our way through the seaweed hedges and anemone beds. "It's been a while since it was just you and me," I said after a while.

"Yeah," Rogue agreed. "Funny; there was a time when it was only *ever* just you and me."

"Now we have Elva, and Marina has agreed to join us. The group is only going to get bigger."

"You ok with that?"

"If it means more ammunition against Raphael, definitely. You know, it's funny… it's easier to be around people here than it is at home."

"I've noticed that," Rogue said, regarding me. "You seem more comfortable."

"I guess it's hard to worry about feeling awkward or saying the wrong thing when you're already worried about trying to stay alive," I laughed. "I have been really anxious about upsetting Elva. Now with Marina I sometimes feel like I'm better off not saying anything at all, you know?"

"You can't think like that. The Guardians will know how important it is to reunite the Heart," Rogue said reasonably.

"They're not going to refuse to help just because of something you said."

"But how do w~" A muffled yell echoing in the distance stopped me flat.

"What was that?" Rogue murmured.

"The party?"

"Too close. Which direction did it come from?" she asked, looking around.

"That way," I pointed. We swam over the hedges, staying hidden as best we could, sneaking through the gardens in search of the sound.

We heard a scream. Rogue and I shared a single terrified glance before we threw away all caution and swam high up over the gardens. "There!" Rogue pointed. A few hedges over from where we had been searching, closer to the middle where the reception hall was, were a group of merpeople. Two of them were grappling.

"Who is that?" I asked. Rogue didn't answer, swimming off at full speed. I immediately followed.

"*Rogue! Ranger! Wait!*" we heard a terrified voice scream out. But we'd already barrelled into the fray. I tackled Rekin to the ground, knocking his axe from his grip, just as Rogue threw herself at Mannix. He batted her aside like she were no more than an irritating fly.

"GET OFF ME!" Rekin roared.

"*REKIN*, STOP!" I yelled back. "WHAT ARE YOU

DOING?"

"That's not Mannix," he growled, retrieving his axe and taking aim, but Marina got there first. She shot a blast of aqua blue light at Mannix, but all he did was laugh.

"The Destroyer," Rogue groaned, getting up.

"I don't understand," Marina gasped, holding the tail necklace at her throat. "Nothing stands against the Heart? Even *now* it won't serve me?"

Rekin circled around. "I found Mannix unconscious in the gardens," he said. "I knew it was close. I tracked it here." The Destroyer with Mannix's face smirked. "I won't let it hurt Morgana."

The Destroyer opened its jaws wide, far wider than the real Mannix could have. It was grotesque. It laughed. On and on, it laughed. "Morgana?" it rasped. "She has no value to me. She was useful for one reason and one reason alone."

"And what was that exactly?" Marina challenged him, moving forward, forming a triangle between her, the Destroyer and Rekin; she armed with her sceptre, he with his axe.

The Destroyer's hands were empty when it exploded into the same cloud of darkness we'd seen when Mannix had attacked it as Morgana, but when it reappeared right in front of Marina, it held a jagged bone dagger, which it swiftly slid between her ribs. "Because she led me right to you," it hissed poisonously.

CHAPTER 16
Questions

§§

Morgana was screaming. I froze. Rogue launched herself at the Destroyer. The Destroyer disappeared into its dark cloud once again, leaving behind it a deep echoing laugh. Marina slowly drifted to the sandy ocean floor, the water around her turning pink and cloudy. Elva leapt to her side. Rekin dropped his axe.

"MARINA! *No, no, no, no, no!*" Morgana cried, holding Marina's face in her hands. "You're going to be ok. I promise, you're going to be alright. We're going to fix this!" she rambled, sobbing. Marina's breathing was coming in short rasps. She raised her hand to her sister's face, trailing a finger along her cheek, before her eyes grew still and the hand dropped to her side. Morgana screamed again, shaking her sister's body fiercely. "Come back! Come back!" she cried weakly through her sobs. The light in the Guardian necklace pulsed one final time before it disappeared completely.

Elva placed her hand on Marina's head, stroking her hair.

The necklace began to glow again. As we watched, the light grew brighter and more vibrant, until it was surrounding Marina's entire body. Then, a beam of the concentrated aqua light shot out of her body and struck Rekin directly in the chest.

None of us moved. I couldn't breathe. I just floated there, watching the spectacle unfold, as more light came from Marina and was absorbed by Rekin. It became so bright I had to shield my eyes, and when it finally died down and I could see again, Marina was gone and Rekin's eyes were glowing white. The Guardian necklace was now around his neck, the fish tail glowing once more.

Rekin blinked and his eyes returned to normal. "What happened?"

"Y-you-" I started.

"-Congratulations Rekin," Elva said, getting up. "You're a Guardian."

Rekin... My dear boy...

Rekin's eyes widened, his jaw falling open. "Liang?"

You have done well, Rekin. You should be proud.

"But I couldn't save you!" he cried out into the night. "I couldn't save *her!* How could I possibly be the Guardian?"

All is as it should be child... Peace.

"Who are you?" he asked. He turned to Rogue and me. "Who is that?"

"Romira," Elva answered. "He and all the Guardians who

came before you are a part of you now."

Rekin looked down at his hands, as though trying to find all these additional people his soul now carried. "Then where is my sister?" Morgana shot at him, finally getting up. "Where is Marina?" Rekin shook his head, at a loss.

Calm yourself. Marina is at peace. Romira's voice was soft and slow. It created an almost sopoforic effect.

The anger in Morgana's eyes died. "Then where is she?"

Marina has moved on, as she was always meant to.

"But Elva said the Guardians stay with you!"

And they do, child… but Marina was never a Guardian.

"What?" Morgana's rage re-emerged. "HOW CAN YOU SAY THAT? She protected the Heart for *twelve years!*"

Peace, child… Morgana stopped short, as though she'd forgotten how to speak. *Let me show you what happened the day Marina came to possess the Heart…*

We felt a great pressure weighing down on us and everything went black. Just as I started to panic when I found I couldn't breathe, the light returned and I inhaled as deeply as I could. I grabbed at Rogue. "Are you ok?"

She nodded. She had one hand on her chest and the other on her stomach; her face slightly green. "I was not expecting that."

"Where are we?" Elva asked, looking around. I followed her gaze. We were in what appeared to be a gladiator arena. The stand on the opposite side was so far away we could barely make out the people sitting in them. The sandy floor was almost white and completely bare.

"This… this is Coral Arena!" Morgana gasped. "My parents built it for the selection of the new Guardian… but it looks brand new?" She seemed confused.

This is the arena as it was the day Marina was named Guardian… the day Liang passed on the Heart.

"We've gone back in time?"

No, child. This is merely a memory.

Behind us, doors opened and Lady Oceana and Lord Morgan were led in, surrounded by a posse of sycophants and guards. "Mother! Father!" Morgana swam forward, but they paid her no attention. It was like she wasn't even there.

They cannot see us. We are simply observers.

"Isn't this a most exciting day!" Lady Oceana squealed with delight. The group of women around her giggled and swam around excitedly.

"Mattara will talk about this day for decades!" Lord Morgan's voice boomed throughout the pavilion. The men cheered and roared in response.

"Oh! We *never* get to see the passing on of the Heart *EVER!*" a woman whined. "Greedy Guardians always keeping the event to themselves!" She fawned over Lord Morgan. "You are so *noble* to share this with all of Mattara!"

"Ew," I said under my breath. Rogue groaned. Morgana looked embarrassed.

"Mother!" a voice rang out. I gasped. It was another Morgana. "Have you seen Marina this morning? I can't find her!"

"She was doing her hair when I saw her this morning, Dear!" she called back. "She'll be along very soon. She wouldn't miss this! And certainly not the opportunity to show off after spending so long getting ready!" Lady Oceana laughed. "Why don't you just *ask* her where she is?"

"She's shut me out!" Morgana complained. "She won't answer me!"

"She wouldn't answer me because she was with the other candidates," the Morgana with us said. She pointed into the arena. "Down there."

"Ooooh!" another woman squealed again. "They're coming!" She mimicked our Morgana, pointing into the arena. At the far end, giant gates had been pulled open and maybe two dozen people had strode into the arena, their heads held high. Each was fully armed and every single one was dressed as though they had just come from Morgana's wedding.

"I thought Guardian selection was about skills?" Rekin said, confused. "This looks like a beauty pageant!"

"Mother and Father wanted everyone to look their best. You'll see their skills, just wait," Morgana told him.

"Wait," Rogue said, holding up a hand. "You were Liang's apprentice."

"Yes?"

"Then where are you?" Elva asked. "You didn't come with Liang?"

Rekin shook his head. Then he nodded. "Yes, I- I did… but I didn't get here in time to see the selection."

"Why not?"

"I had to-"

His answer was cut short as Lord Morgan came to the edge of the pavilion looking out over the arena to address the amassed crowd. "WELCOME!" he called to them. "To the must see event of the season! FOR *ALL* SEASONS!" The crowd clapped and cheered. "Never before have the people of Mattara had the privilege of witnessing the passing on of the Heart and the naming of a new Guardian!" More cheers. "I invite you all to bear witness as the candidates show you just what they are made of!" I was deafened as the eruption of noise as the crowd positively screamed their excitement.

"Who chose the candidates?" Elva asked.

"What do you mean?" Morgana asked.

"The people in the arena? How did they come to be there? Who chose them?"

"Oh… My parents did, I guess?"

Elva shook her head, angry and confused. "The Heart is not meant to be restricted like that. No wonder Marina's abilities were so stunted."

"It wasn't meant to be her… She was just the best option

presented to the Heart," Morgana whispered, now understanding the implications of her parents choosing those who were to compete for the Guardianship. "There she is!" She pointed down into the area. We recognised the scaled headdress and pearl and shell sceptre instantly. They were the same ones she bore when we first met her, but this time the scales of the headdress came down her face, forming a mask around her eyes, and her tail was a shimmering gold. "Mother and father didn't recognise her… Her face was covered; she had masked her tail."

"But you knew," Rekin said. "Didn't you?"

"I knew the moment I saw her," Morgana whispered back, looking at her eighteen year old self by her mother, watching all the candidates circle around the arena.

The look of shock on the younger Morgana's face was clear, but Oceana and Morgan remained ignorant. "My Lord and Lady!" They turned to find an elderly cecaelia entering the pavilion, flanked by four guards. "I present the Guardian!"

"Liang!" Rekin gasped.

"Liang! You took so long Dear!" Lady Oceana crooned. "We're *so glad* you didn't miss anything!"

The adoring fans surrounding the Lord and Lady clapped appreciatively. "They're *so* thoughtful!" one of them sighed.

"This isn't right, my Lady," Liang said to her. The fans instantly went silent. Clearly *no one* questioned the Lord and

Lady of Mattara. "The Heart is not ready to move on." There was a nervous giggle somewhere.

"Liang *please!* We discussed this!" Lord Morgan said cheerfully, clapping them on the shoulder. "You have worked long and hard all these decades serving the Heart! It's time for a break! You've *earned it!*" He put a lot of emphasis in these last words, like he was sending Liang a deeper message… a threat.

"Morgan knew this wasn't right!" Elva said, shaking her head. "How could he think any good would come of this?"

"Liang had been named Guardian almost a century before Morgan was even born," Rekin pointed out. "Its power, its importance; the reverence for the role of the Guardian was completely lost on him."

"It's all about the show…" Morgana said softly as her father returned to the pavilion banister.

"LET THE GAMES BEGIN!" Morgan bellowed to the mass of mermaids, naiads, triakis and cecaelia. The shouts of the crowd doubled.

Throughout the hours that followed we watched all manner of skills. Daggers were thrown, magicks were tested, battles were fought with sword, staff and trident; they were set upon by various sea creatures and had to dodge multiple hazards like jagged sea urchins and poisonous corals.

I balked when a tremendous rumbling started below our feet and the arena floor started to separate, until a jagged crack had appeared down the centre. From within the darkness something stirred and several long, dark tentacles snuck out and started feeling around the arena.

"Oh *no*," I shivered. Giant shellfish.

"It's horrible, isn't it?" Morgana said. "My parents lost twenty seven guards getting it here from the Great Chasm," she told them. Rogue's mouth dropped open as several of the candidates launched themselves at the creeping tentacles. Instantly the tension in the water changed. The tentacles shot out and started ripping candidates from the arena, down into the dungeon below the floor as shouts, howls and boos echoed from the watching crowd.

"I can't look!" I squeaked, covering my eyes. I heard the shouts, the gasps, the yells, as well as multiple squishy *splats* that I was thrilled to not be witnessing the cause of. "Tell me when it's over!"

"The floor is closing!" I heard Rogue yell over the noise of the crowd. I opened my eyes in time to see the final tentacle slide back below the surface of the arena and the gaping hole in the ground disappear.

"*CONGRATULATIONS FINALISTS!*" Lord Morgan yelled to them from the pavilion banister. "You have done well to have come this far!" I could see Marina breathing heavily as she struggled to remain upright, the sceptre hanging by her side, blood from a cut on her arm leeching into the water around her. "I PRESENT TO YOU, *LIANG!* OUR OUTGOING

GUARDIAN!"

Elva gasped. "Such disrespect! To be a Guardian is the be *the Guardian*, you don't *name* them!" she spat in outrage. "And calling them the outgoing Guardian like they have no value?"

"To them, they don't," Rekin cut her off gravely as Liang came forward. The Guardian stared into Lord Morgan's eyes. He nodded encouragingly, a grand smile on his face, but his eyes were cold and empty.

Liang looked down slightly, touching the tail fin necklace. "All will be well," they said quietly. "All will be put right."

"*Yes, Liang!*" Lord Morgan said, leading him to the edge of the pavilion. "Everything is as it should be!" Liang swam over the railing and into the open water of the arena. As they moved closer to the remaining candidates, each of them lined themselves up in front of Liang, chins up, ready for the scrutiny.

"Only eight left," Rogue whispered, forgetting that we couldn't be heard.

Rekin looked behind us. I turned as well, but there was nothing there. "What's wrong?" I asked him.

He shook his head, refusing to meet my eye. "Nothing." He moved forward to watch the selection. I followed him, frowning. Liang was swimming along the line of candidates, almost like they were pacing in front of the line. We watched curiously. "It's like they're delaying on purpose!" Rekin said.

"What is Liang delaying for?" Elva asked.

Rekin didn't answer. He silently watched as Liang approached each candidate in turn, touching a finger to each of their foreheads. When Liang touched them, each candidate let out a sigh of relief, as their torn bodies and aching muscles were healed.

Marina was the last in line. Liang turned their head ever so slightly, as though they were going to turn back to the pavilion. Liang seemed to change their mind though, as instead, they made their way towards Marina.

There was a knock at the door to the pavilion. No one moved to open it. Neither Lord Morgan and Lady Oceana, nor any of their loyal followers even showed any indication that they heard it.

Liang was close to Marina now. They were reaching for her forehead.

The door creaked open. My curiosity got the better of me. I looked over my shoulder.

CHAPTER 17

...& Answers

§§

There was a gasp from Elva and the whole crowd erupted with cheers as a bright aqua light flooded the arena... at the very moment a young Rekin crossed the threshold and entered the pavillion.

"Rekin!" I exclaimed, turning back to our Rekin. Morgana, Rogue and Elva all looked over at us curiously. "It was Rekin!" I pointed to the young triakis, waiting anxiously by the door.

Elva gasped again. "The Heart shone the moment he entered! It was *never* reacting to Marina at all!"

Rekin looked at a loss. "I never knew," he mumbled. "I- I never knew why... why I could hear..."

It was always you, my boy... I knew the Heart would find its way to you... in time.

We watched as Liang lifted the necklace from their neck and place it around Marina's. She raised her arms to the crowd, sceptre in hand, then lifted her hand to her face and removed the mask, finally revealing herself. Gasps and cries of shock rang throughout Coral Arena.

"MARINA!" Lady Oceana screeched, holding her hands to her face, before immediately throwing them into the air and turning her screech into a cheer. "*My daughter!* My daughter has done it! My daughter Marina is the *Guardian!* OH, WELL DONE DARLING!"

"PEOPLE OF MATTARA!" Lord Morgan called to the cheering crowd. "May I introduce to you, out next Guardian, *Lady Marina of Medina!*" The crowd's cheers raised tenfold. He shot a concerned look at his wife, who shook her head jerkily.

Liang swam back to the pavilion, coming up and over the railing and passing us closely, ignoring the crowd. They crossed directly to Rekin, who came toward Liang eagerly. We watched Liang shake their head and raise a hand. "Liang is telling me we'll talk later," our Rekin told us. Then, Liang moved to leave the pavilion and as they placed an arm around Rekin's shoulders, we watched a spark cross from their fingertips and into the young Rekin's body, giving his skin an opalescent glow. "I didn't notice that," our Rekin said, puzzled.

Everything went dark again in an instant, deep and oppressive. Then lights popped into existence and we found ourselves once again in the gardens of South-East Point. "You didn't feel anything?" Elva asked Rekin, ignoring the phenomenon. "Nothing at all?"

"Nothing," he said, shaking his head.

You see Rekin... You have been the Guardian for a very long time... You simply didn't have possession of the Heart to complete the connection.

"Romira?"

Hello Rekin. I am sorry I was not able to guide you as I have other Guardians thus far, but I promise, you are not alone.

"Why could I only hear you after Liang died?"

I remained bound to Liang. They had served the heart for over a century; far longer than any before them. They deserved the same loyalty. While no one knew you were the Guardian; while you did not possess the Heart, you were safe in a way they were not. Despite no longer possessing the Heart, Liang remained in grave danger due to the magicks many in Mattara believed they retained. I could not leave Liang defenceless.

"But Liang was killed anyway!" Rekin exclaimed. "You couldn't protect them even when it counted!"

I can only act through the Heart. My connection to Liang's mind remained, but I was trapped between all three of you. It left my abilities in a loop I could not control.

"So he died... and it left you able to communicate with me easier?"

It was difficult. I tried many times before I was able to

break through. Even then all I could do was urge you to find Morgana, to protect her from the Destroyer, who sought to use her to find Marina… and my Heart.

"You sent Rekin to me?" Morgana asked.

I did. By many twists of fate you and your sister still became bound to the Heart. I would see to it that you were safe as best I could.

"Where is the Destroyer now?" I asked. "Where did it go?"

Granddaughter… I cannot tell you what I do not know. This Destroyer… it is unknown to me; alien to this world. It is both of here, yet not of here. The power of the Heart does not affect it. I have searched ever since it appeared, but I cannot see it.

You must return home. Another voice cut in.

"Liang?" Rekin said. "Home?"

Yes, you must return home; one final time.

Rekin rubbed his forehead, then ran his hands down his whole face, stopping at the chin as he thought. "Yes… I understand," he finally said. "One last time."

"We aren't going *anywhere* yet!" Morgana piped up. "My sister is *dead* and my husband has disappeared! There is work to be done *here!*"

I looked away in shame. "We know, Morgana," Rogue answered. "We promise we'll find Mannix."

"I'll never be able to forgive myself for Marina's death,"

Rekin told her. "I promise you, you will not lose Mannix too."

Morgana's shoulders drooped, all pretence of strength gone. Elva went to her side and held her arm. "We won't leave you," she promised.

Morgana fought to control her sobs as wave after wave of sorrow washed over her. "I found Mannix back this way," Rekin told her, and they steadily made their way back towards the reception hall, where, by the sound of it, the party was still in full swing.

"They don't know," Morgana said weakly. "She's *gone* and they don't know…"

As I passed a flowered kelp bed, I paused, noticing a black tail protruding from it. "Over here!" I yelled out. Rekin and Rogue were at my side in seconds, helping me pull Mannix's bruised, still body from the seaweed. I placed my head to his chest. "He's alive!"

Rekin reached forward and touched Mannix's forehead, who immediately lurched forward. His eyes flew open and he started coughing. "THE DESTROYER!" he yelled.

"It's gone, Mannix! Calm down!" I yelled back. "The Destroyer is gone… for now."

"What happened?" he asked, as Morgana dropped to his side and wrapped her arms around him. She immediately started to sob.

♠

Marina's funeral was almost grander than Morgana's wedding. The largest chapel in Medina had been covered in night lilies, a beautiful navy bloom with glowing golden stamens coming out of the throat. A parade of those paying tribute to Marina's memory followed Lady Oceana, Lord Morgan, Mannix and Morgana down the main street of Medina and into the chapel for the service. There were so many people in attendance, the doors and windows had been thrown open so those who couldn't physically fit inside could still be involved.

I was sitting on a ledge outside the top left window, watching Morgana in the front row. Rekin, Elva and Rogue sat along the ledge, listening silently as the priest inside delivered Marina's final rites. I closed my eyes as he finished the final prayer, and as the congregation began to sing, I got up and swam back down to the street. The others followed.

"Do we say goodbye?" Rogue asked.

"No," Rekin answered. "There will be a lot happening, particularly here in the Capitol over the next few days with Marina's death. We have to make the most of the distraction and leave while no one is paying any attention to us."

"What about you?" I asked. "Surely there will be balls and parades celebrating the new Guardian?"

"No," he answered immediately. "Besides us Morgana is the only one who knows I'm a Guardian and after what happened to Liang and Marina, she won't tell anyone what she knows. As far as anyone is aware… the Heart of Peace is gone."

"Which leaves us free to search for the Destroyer and bind it," Elva nodded authoritatively.

We had been planning our next move throughout the days it took to plan Marina's funeral and we had decided on a three step plan to get us home. First, we had to return to the home Rekin had shared with Liang. When we asked exactly what we were returning for, Rekin wouldn't explain, only saying it would be pointless leaving Mattara if we didn't go.

Next, we had to find the Destroyer and neutralise the threat it posed to Mattara. Like Ariannah, it was seemingly impervious to the Heart's magic, but that was when Marina was wielding it. Elva had devised a plan. If Rekin and Elva's combined Hearts didn't work, then Elva would weave the same spell she had for Ariannah to place the Destroyer into a deep sleep. "The Destroyer is powerful, but I'm absolutely certain that with Rekin, I can do it again."

Finally, they had to find the next mirror. They had spent almost an entire day poring over the Ventura maps and the riddle. "How are these even *surviving* underwater?" I asked incredulously when Rogue pulled them from her bag.

"No idea," she had answered. "Just be thankful for small favours and don't ask too many questions. Ah! Here's the riddle: *the third where nature is lush and full of life, where they receive the most light; the pack will demand its due respect, for their triumphs and their might."*

"I'm sorry, pack of *what* exactly?" Elva had questioned fearfully.

"Let's worry about where they are before we start worrying about what they are," I had answered. "We can't go home without knowing where we're going next, not with two pieces of the Heart."

"Nature is everywhere," Rekin had declared. "It doesn't exactly narrow it down." He was analysing the blueprints of Ventura Castle.

"It's not the same in our world, Rekin," I told him. "Ventura is very nature-rich, but each of these mirrors is in the castle; a building. The nature description is more relevant than it appears." I stood by him, both of us going over each floor. "The sunrooms have a lot of light?" I suggested.

"We searched both of them when we were looking for the Valerian mirror," Rogue pointed out. "If they were there, we would've found it."

"Is a conservatory the same in your world as it is in Valeria?" Elva suddenly asked, pointing to a room on the fourth floor. "It's an indoor greenhouse?"

"Where the location is chosen for maximum sun exposure and it's kept at a hotter temperature to promote plant growth!" Rogue said rapidly, her excitement obvious as she put the riddle down and came over to the map. "Fourth floor…" She raised her eyebrow at me knowingly. "My theory is proving true, it seems!"

"Your theory?" Rekin questioned.

"Rogue thinks there's one mirror on each floor," I told him. "We found one mirror on the third floor and the other on the fifth. If this mirror *is* in fact on the fourth floor, then that makes the mirror search easier, because we can rule out searching entire floors," I explained.

"That would definitely make things easier for finding the other mirrors should the theory prove true," he had agreed, nodding.

Now, here we were; one step into the three step plan. With a final glance at the chapel and the mass of mourners, the four of us turned and headed for the North gate.

CHAPTER 18

The Great Chasm

§§

"No."

"Not a chance!"

"There is no way?"

"Not happening."

"You have a death wish."

"Are you trying to kill us?"

We were near the edge of the Mattaran map; at the north-eastern corner of the world. We could barely hear each other over the roar of the water around us. Rekin stood before Elva, Rogue and I, smiling broadly, as we stared back with shock, indignation and pure terror on our faces.

Rekin stood on the edge of a precipice; a long, low, rocky wall directly behind him holding back a monstrous whirlpool. The vortex was so large, I couldn't see the other side, yet Rekin was grinning like he was the tour guide at a zoo, sharing the newest attraction, and like many attractions at a zoo, this one was likely to kill us if we got too close.

"This is the only safe way in," Rekin declared.

"*Safe?*" Elva scoffed. She pointed aggressively at the giant whirlpool. "That's the Chasm cavern entrance all over again!"

"Yes," Rekin agreed. "And *just like* the Chasm cavern, *this* is the only entrance, and it's not going to hurt you. It's *harmless!*"

"*Harmless?*" Elva yelled.

"Well, it's not like we can drown," I pointed out.

"That's the spirit!" Rekin smiled. "I'll see you other the other side!" And then he swam high above us, spun his body around and dived straight down through the centre of the whirlpool.

"Well, that was interesting," Rogue said, as I stared, unblinking at the spot where Rekin had disappeared.

"Yes, it was nice knowing him," Elva said quickly, swimming away. "Rest in peace, Rekin!"

"*ELVA!*" Rogue and I called.

"Oh, come *on!*" she protested, turning back to us. "You *cannot* be serious?"

"We'll be right there with you," I promised, linking my arm through hers. Rogue did the same on the other side and we slowly led Elva to the open ocean above the whirlpool. The closer we came, the more she struggled.

"Together?" Rogue asked. I nodded. Elva shook her head, her face white. "Go!" I unnecessarily held my breath as we dove down into the swirling water. Immediately Elva's arm was ripped from my grasp as we were pulled apart by the rapidly moving current. I couldn't see anything but white foam or hear anything but the rush of the bubbles. The longer we were in the violent waves, the faster the movement became until I felt something bony hit me in the side. I immediately clamped onto it and held on as the water moved faster and faster.

Finally, there was a loud suctioning noise and a high *pop!* and I was spat out the other side, landing with a hard *thump* on a giant pink sea sponge, my limbs completely entangled with Rogue and Elva's.

"HARMLESS MY LEFT WING!" Elva screamed, throwing Rogue's tail out of her face, causing her be thrown off the sea sponge. She gasped. "*Sorry!*"

"I'm fine," Rogue grumbled.

"How was the ride?" Rekin asked, grinning broadly. "Right this way!" He bowed deeply, raising an arm to direct us through the cavern path. I took Elva's hand and helped her down from the sea sponge.

"Where are we?" Rogue asked.

"The pools led us back to the other side of Mattara. We are deep in the undersea here."

"Ok, *next* question!" Elva demanded. "Those tide pools are one way only. If that's how we got in, *how* exactly are we getting out?"

I stopped. "I didn't think of that."

"Don't worry," Rekin assured us. "The way out is a lot easier than the way in."

"Then why didn't we use that way to get here in the first place?" Rogue asked.

"It would have taken a lot longer and the way we'll take to get out is *far* more dangerous when you try to take that way to get in."

"What makes it any safer on the way out?" I asked.

"The element of surprise," Rekin answered simply. He smiled at us cheerfully.

We all stared stonily back. "He's going to get us all killed," Elva grumbled.

"Well luckily we were already halfway to doing that ourselves!" I sighed.

We continued to follow Rekin through the caverns. They were larger than the ones we had found Marina in. I was starting to suspect where we were when I saw shells growing out of the walls, with tiny tentacles exploring the water just outside of them. I shuddered deeply to myself, but didn't mention it. "Where exactly are we going?" I asked instead.

"It's not much further. This way." Rekin pointed above us, where the ceiling of the cavern was riddled with large holes. He selected a specific one and led us inside. "Welcome to my home."

It really did look and feel like a home. Beautiful shells

covered the walls, hand carved pictures sat on stone tables and benches, soft, squishy sea sponge sofas had been grown around a large hydro-thermal vent and shelves upon shelves of books covered the walls. "Wow," I exhaled.

"This is beautiful!"

"You lived here?"

Rekin nodded. "With Liang, for ten years of Guardianship; then another two weeks and three days after…"

"What happened?"

Rekin went to the bookcase and started running his fingers along the volumes. "Liang had been deteriorating from the moment they gave up the Heart of Peace," he began quietly. "When we came home, Liang brought me here, to these books, and insisted that I read every single one I hadn't yet read. When I asked why Liang simply said '*It is the duty of the apprentice to obey the master*'.

"I would read so late into the night, desperate to find what it is he wanted me to know." He shook his head in distress, looking to the large purple sea sponge by the bookshelves. "I was asleep when Liang arrived home one day, bleeding. They had been attacked out in the caverns."

"I took Liang to their room… and they died in my arms. Their body glowed just like Marina's had and when the light disappeared… so had they. Liang told me what would happen their body when they died; it didn't make me any more prepared to see it," he finished sadly.

"You were with Liang almost your entire life?" Rogue asked. "How old were you when you were apprenticed to him?"

"Four. I had lost my parents and was taken to live with my aunt in Medina. She worked in the Coral Palace. While we were there one day I was racing through the halls and I ran into Liang," a smile crossed Rekin's face as he reminisced. "My aunt was so angry I thought her eyes were going to pop out, but Liang said I showed promise and would she allow me to be apprenticed to them. Liang was my family from then on."

"Why did you need to come back here, Rekin?" Rogue asked. "To say goodbye?"

"I lost my parents as a child, my aunt gave me away to the first person who asked and I'm about to leave the world that has been my home my entire life," he answered icily. "I'm not exactly the sentimental type."

"Then why are we here?" I asked.

"For this." He reached into the end bookshelf and removed a clam shell the size of a large jewellery box. He opened it and pulled out a black, leather bound journal.

"What is that?" I asked.

"*HOW DID YOU GET THAT?*" Rogue yelled at the same time.

"You had it all along?" Elva gasped.

"Have I missed something?" I frowned.

Rekin looked sheepish. "Liang handed over the book on the day of the Guardian selection… but he left with it too."

Everything clicked into place. "The book from South-East Point! It was stolen from the Coral Palace!" I exclaimed. "You-you were late to the selection because you were *stealing* it!"

"Liang couldn't let this fall into the wrong hands, but people kept far too close an eye for them to do anything. Me, however… I was the apprentice boy; not a threat and not important enough to pay attention to."

"So the Destroyer started killing and kidnapping people-" Elva began.

"-And everyone just assumed it stole the book," Rogue finished. Rekin nodded.

"May I?" Rekin handed me the book. "Have you read this?" I asked.

"I can't. It's blank to me."

"Marina must have been right; only the Royce line can read it," Rogue said.

I looked at the cover curiously. The leather was covered in knots and ridges. Written in red across the front was the title: *The Journal of Vinderas Ulysses Ivanya Bundan.* "A journal? A *journal* is what Raphael can't get his hands on?"

"As it turns out…" a deep, sickly voice drawled. "…he can."

CHAPTER 19

Havoc

§§

Immediately the tail fin and elven necklaces began to glow a vivid pink and aqua blue and both Elva and Rekin shot a powerful blast of energy at the Destroyer, which was still wearing Mannix's face. It disappeared in an eruption of darkness before the blasts could land.

"Ranger! *Go!*" Rogue screamed. "We'll cover you!" I didn't need to be told twice. I swam as fast as I could, urging myself to go faster. As I swam I felt my body tingle all over and I shot forward with an additional burst of speed. My arms in front of me were now almost white and my hair felt thicker and heavier than before.

Behind me I could hear shouts and crashes as the Destroyer attacked again and again. There was a burst of darkness in front of me, but before it could take shape, I dove below it and kept swimming, barely losing speed with the change of direction.

"RANGER! *WAIT!*"

"Rekin, we can't stop!"

"*YOU DON'T UNDERSTAND!*"

It was too late. I'd barreled through one of the cave entrances and learned it was actually an exit, finding myself surrounded by monstrous shellfish larger than the Coral Palace itself. Hundreds of tentacles were snaking their way through the water around me. I froze for half a second.

"DO NOT SLOW DOWN!" Rekin bellowed. "Go *through* them, not above!" I caught Rogue's eye and as she saw my transformation, she and Elva complied, their mermaid tails lengthening and slimming down to that of a triakis. Within moments we were surrounded by masses of tentacles, dodging and weaving through them like they were jungle vines.

The Destroyer moved just as quickly, exploding into inky darkness whenever a tentacle got too close, only to reappear in front of us seconds later, creating yet another series of obstacles. We rose to the challenge, our triakis tails never failing us.

"*Not much further!*" Rekin yelled. "The shellfish aren't as dense up ahead!" I had noticed the tentacles weren't as thick. I pressed forward, bursting through the other side and into the ocean valley that was the Great Chasm.

The moment I was through, the darkness exploded in front me again. I didn't slow down, but this time when I reached the cloud, the Destroyer had begun to form within it.

I hit it head on, sending the both of us head over fin, but nothing was going to stop me from holding onto that book. I held it with an iron grip, whipping my tail through the water and knocking the Destroyer away from me.

It roared, almost dislocating its jaw to do so and launched itself back at me. I prepared to engage, my hands glowing green. The Destroyer came for me. It had just come within range, when a huge shadow fell over the top of us, causing it to pause and look at us. Above us was a mammoth fish moving slowly through the Great Chasm.

"Coelacanth!" Rekin puffed, reaching me. Elva and Rogue were right behind him. The fish turned and came towards us, mouth open.

"Are coelacanth one of those *carnivorous* fish you mentioned?" I called to the Destroyer.

It growled back, then it shot a web of darkness at the mouth of the creature. It roared back, shaking its head back and forth. Rekin took the opportunity to follow suit, following up the Destroyer's attack with a bright blue blast of his own. The moment the coelacanth began to turn, he redirected his efforts to the Destroyer, who had turned its attention back to us. The Destroyer kept coming, like it couldn't feel a thing.

"ELVA, *HELP ME!*" Rekin yelled. Elva came forward and raised her hands to the Destroyer, joining her pink to his blue. It faltered, but only for a moment, before it redoubled its efforts.

"*It's not going to work!*"

"Time for plan B?"

Elva nodded, and she and Rekin switched positions so she was in front. "Attacks to harm won't work! You need to will it to *sleep!*"

Rekin nodded, closing his eyes in concentration for just a second. When he opened them, his eyes were white and his whole body began to glow. Elva added her power to his, their pink and blue combining to purple as they circled the Destroyer, forcing it to the ocean floor.

"You cannot defeat me!" it rasped, fighting the power of the Hearts. "I… am… *HAVOC!*"

"*SLEEP!*" Elva commanded, moving closer. Rekin mimicked her. Steadily they came closer to the Destroyer.

Its eyes drooped and slowly, it collapsed on the ground. "I am… Havoc…" it whispered, before falling silent.

Rogue and I joined Elva and Rekin, their bodies no longer glowing, their eyes returning to normal. "Havoc," Rekin repeated. "The Destroyer has a name?"

"Apparently so," Elva answered. "Where do we leave it?"

"You're sure it won't wake?"

"It shouldn't as long as the Hearts survive."

Rekin considered his options. "Home," he finally answered. "We leave the Destroyer… *Havoc*, at home. Even if it were to wake up it would have a hard time getting out of the Great Chasm," he said.

"Agreed," I answered. "Better here than anywhere else."

"Who will protect it?" Rogue asked. "Someone has to keep watch. We can't just leave it alone."

Rekin smirked, looking up at the still circling coelacanth. "Leave that to me."

♠

Back in the Capitol, we were meeting with Lord Morgan and Lady Oceana… and they were not happy. "How *dare* you come here and suggest such a thing!"

"After we just lost our *daughter!*"

"Your daughter wouldn't have been placed in such a situation had you not forced Liang to pass on the Heart before their time was done," Rekin said forcefully. "That responsibility lies… with *you.*"

Morgan looked apoplectic with rage. "*HOW DARE YOU!*" Lady Oceana shrieked.

"*Mother!*" Morgana snapped. Her parents turned to her and Mannix. She held Marina's scepter in her hands. "You and Father have not made choices that reflect what is best for Mattara," she scolded them. "This gives the both of you the chance to step down without the entire world learning what you have done; saving face and finally doing what is right by our people!"

"You would usurp us, Daughter?" Morgan breathed

dangerously.

"Never, Father," she answered innocently, before her voice turned harsh. "But I *will* take up the mantle of Lady of Mattara readily when the people learn that you forced the Heart of Peace to move on before its time, forced it into the hands of the wrong person which lead to Marina's death *and* had the true Guardian killed!"

"You couldn't *possibly!*" Oceana gasped in horror, one hand on her heart, the other clutching Morgan's arm.

"Tell the world what you've done?" Morgana asked. "I would never." She pointed to us. "But they would." I nodded in agreement.

"*We will never bow to you!*" Morgan hissed.

"We don't expect you to," Rekin growled, completely calm. "But the Hearts exist to protect the worlds of Ventura~"

"~And if that means we need to use them to protect Mattara *from* you, we will," Elva finished, the necklaces at their throats pulsing in synchronicity.

Lady Oceana stared fearfully. "How could you *do* this?"

"We could ask you the same," Rogue shot back.

"Do the right thing," I urged. "You step down, announce to Mattara that with Morgana now ready to lead and Marina having died you are ready to step down and let her and Mannix take control of the affairs of the world while you enjoy a well deserved retirement." I sneered. "Think of the parties you'll be able to throw for *that.*"

CHAPTER 20

The Journal of Vinderas Ulysses Ivanya Bundan

§§

"MAY I PRESENT TO YOU, LADY MORGANA AND LORD MANNIX!" The crowd outside the Coral Palace clapped and cheered.

Morgana and Mannix stood before the people of Mattara. Morgana had declined her mother's tiara, instead adorning herself with Marina's headdress and sceptre. Mannix had also refused to take the crown from Morgan. "I'm not royalty and I won't pretend I am," he had said simply.

"We promise to ensure every decision will be made for the betterment of Mattara! To be leaders open to change and innovation! Ready and prepared to do whatever it takes to keep our people safe and our world, prosperous!" Lady Morgana declared to the Medina public, speaking fluently and eloquently. The people clapped.

"She was made for this," I said, smiling.

"Reminds me of her university speeches," Rekin said. "She never does things by halves; forever a ten out of ten."

"LET THE CELEBRATIONS *BEGIN!*" The former Lord Morgan yelled, throwing his fist into the air. The crowd erupted again.

Morgana and Mannix left the balcony overlooking the city square and came over to us. "That was nerve-wracking!" Mannix gasped, wiping his forehead. "How am I meant to do that every other day?"

"It certainly *won't* be every other day," Morgana answered, linking her arm through his. "I have no plans to lead as my parents did."

"Well, that's certainly a relief. I don't like public speaking."

"And I take it that has nothing to do with being a Lord?" Rogue asked him, winking, before bowing low. Mannix shook his head.

"Your life is just beginning. Don't jump in with such negativity," I advised him. "It's not healthy for you or for Morgana. You're going to need each other in the weeks and months to come."

"I'll take care of her as I always have," he promised us.

"I'll hold you to that," Rekin said, shaking his hand.

"Good luck you two," Rogue said, hugging Morgana. "You'll do great." Morgana gave us all one last smile, standing beside Mannix as we left the Coral Palace for the last time.

At the city gates, we had some unexpected visitors. "Rekin," Shoal nodded. "We're ready." Shoal, Maxima, Mortima and Naira were shoulder to shoulder, an empty carriage behind them.

"Thank you for coming," Rekin greeted him, shaking his hand.

"You know each other?" I asked curiously.

"Not exactly," Rekin answered. "We needed someone to guard Havoc. The Heart thought who better than those who have battled it before?"

"You're going to keep watch over the Destroyer?" Rogue asked, worried. "Are you sure?"

"We are sure," Shoal nodded. "With Inkan village safe and the dangers of the Centre having abated, we are pleased to have such purpose again."

"And I will greatly appreciate the peace and quiet of the Great Chasm," Naira spoke up. "I know why it lures so many of my kin. I will find it most pleasing."

"Peace, Brother," Rekin said, taking Shoal's hand once more. Shoal nodded, and the four of them swam into the city.

"Good luck everyone," I whispered.

"Take care at the tide pools!" Elva muttered under her breath in a sing song voice, clearly thrilled it wasn't her this time.

"Are you ready?" Rekin asked.

"Ready for what?" Rogue said. Rekin grinned mischievously and the tail fin necklace began to glow. "What are you doing? *REKIN!*"

When the light died down, we were in the middle of an open sandy field, empty ocean all around us. "Where are we?" I asked.

"Mummy!" a small voice cried out.

"Lani?" I gasped, turning to the voice. "*LANI!*"

"*RANGER!*" she squealed back. "MUMMY COME QUICK!" Ramona was out the front door in a flash, as Lani leapt into my arms and hugged me fiercely.

"Hi kiddo!" Rogue laughed, as Lani jumped from my arms into hers.

"Hello beautiful girl!" Elva said, getting her turn.

"Who's that?" Lani asked loudly as Ramona joined us.

"Yes," she said. "Who have you brought with you, girls?"

"My name is Rekin," Rekin introduced himself, as Lani reached out and grabbed his Guardian necklace in her small pudgy hand.

"This is pret-oh!" she gasped as the necklace began to glow.

Hello Granddaughter.

"*WHO IS THAT?*" Lani squealed, holding her ears. "HE'S IN MY HEAD!"

"Who is that?" Ramona asked fearfully.

I am your history, just as you are my future.

"Romira?" she exhaled.

Hello Granddaughter.

"You," she said to Rekin. "You're the Guardian!" Rekin nodded, his eyes shining.

"Who is he, Mummy?" Lani yelled, her hands still over her ears.

"He is our many times Great Grandfather, Lani," Ramona answered, picking her up. "He is a part of the Heart of Peace, so we can talk to him."

"WOW!" she said loudly, her hands dropping.

It brings me great joy to know you have found peace here in Mattara.

"Thank you, Grandfather," Ramona said, her voice catching.

Where is the book?

"The book?" I repeated. "It's here." I pulled out *The Journal of Vinderas Ulysses Ivanya Bundan* from my bag.

Open it, child.

I looked around the group nervously, then opened the cover and began to read. *"Established 236,*

"I begin this journal in the hopes that all the years I have to live to do not disappear into oblivion. To be immortal can be a curse, for what value does life have if it is potentially infinite?"

"Immortal?" Elva said.

"To live forever," Rekin told her.

"I *know* that," she snapped. "I'm part *elf*. Keep reading."
I flipped through some pages.

"*Year 407,*

"*It has been a long time since I lost my mother, but I continue to think of her. My father becomes all the more vindictive as the witches' anger grows~*"

"~Witches~!" Rogue gasped.

"*~I have never seen him with so little mercy. I cannot abide his behaviour. I have met a woman, and the love I feel for her rivals anything and everything I have ever felt for anyone else. If my father's war were to lead to her harm… I could never forgive myself.*"

I turned a page. "*Year 549,*

"*She is returned to me. After so long waiting, she has returned. Like myself, age has not touched her. She insists our love cannot be, that she cannot remain here with me. I move to speak with her father tomorrow.*

"*The war has escalated, with many deaths on both sides. I sought divine help. I found myself praying in the church, begging the creator to intervene. Never in my wildest dreams did I expect a response and never did I expect who answered my call.*

"*It was her father. I had never met our creator, but I had met her father… and the two were one and the same. She came with him, my beloved, the daughter of Romira~*"

"~NO WAY!" Rogue and Elva yelled in unison.

"Romana had a relationship with someone from Mattara," realised.

"We don't *have* immortals here," Rekin said, confused.

Keep reading…

I nodded, turning to the final page. *"Romira will not interfere with the choices of his world, but he has offered me the chance to leave this place; escape my father. I am torn. My love is all I have ever dreamed of in all these years of loneliness trapped within my father's palace.*

"All I think of is her face. It lights up my entire being; pushing away the darkness in my soul, but I fear of what will come of the world if I abandon it. I cannot leave my people."

Move to the end.

I heeded Romira's instruction. *"Year 553,*

"The war has ended this very evening. The people wanted to see me crowned, but I cannot accept. The witch Ulyanna has been chosen and I have supported her claim. With her coronation I hope the world finally sees peace.

"It is something I cannot commit to witnessing however. My love has sought me out again and with the war over, I will not lose her again. I follow her, leaving this world to likely never return. Romira has made the arrangements. He honours me by welcoming me into his home… as a son."

"If Vinderas came through to our world… then where is he?" Rogue asked. "Romana never married. There is no one on her branch of the family tree. She raised Raven and

Raphael's child Rachael all alone."

"Which means he either never came through after all~" Rekin started.

"~Or something happened to him before he could marry Romana," Elva finished for him.

"I don't understand," Ramona said, shaking her head. "This book is apparently so dangerous that should Raphael ever get his hands on it, all is lost… but how is anything in it relevant?"

"It tells us there are players on the board we didn't know about," I answered. "It tells us that there is far more to learn about Ventura."

"Surely, Romira, you can clarify this?" Ramona cried. "Surely you know what happened! This is your Heart with your soul and your memories! Why will you not tell us who this Vinderas is and why he matters? Surely you can tell me where my mother is!"

I am a fractured piece of a whole, Ramona. The process of pulling oneself apart causes damage that cannot be repaired. I will do whatever I am able to aid in this quest, but I cannot share what I do not know. I can promise you however, that your mother is not lost.

"How could you know that?" I asked as shock crossed Ramona's face.

I have no answers beyond that which I have already given. I know she is alive.

"If she is," Rogue said. "We'll find her."

Yes, I believe you will.

"First we have to get home," I said. "Ramona, do you know where the mirror is?"

Ramona led us inside and sat us down at the table. "There is no mirror to go back," she told us with a sigh, shaking her head.

"What do you mean there's no mirror!" Rogue groaned.

"Do you remember when you first arrived?" Ramona asked. "Lani said you came from the High Place?"

"Yeah?" I nodded, not sure where she was going with this.

"What do you think is above the water here?" she went on. "We're underwater… Do you think there is land above us?"

"What do you mean, Ramona?" Rekin asked her. "There is *nothing* above us. Our entire world is situated underwater. That's the boundary of the world of Mattara; there is nothing else."

"Exactly," Ramona nodded, a small smile playing on her lips.

"So you're saying… if… if we break the surface of the water up… up there," I began, pointing above us. "We'll be breaking the surface… of the spa on the fifth floor?"

"I don't know how it works exactly," Ramona told us. "But yes, that is the way back to Ventura estate." In seconds we were outside and gazing up as far as we could see. "The only way you're going to know is if you go up there."

There was a drawn-out moment's silence, before Rogue breathed in and groaned again loudly. "Let's do it," I breathed.

I took Elva's hand as Rogue took Rekin's. I didn't know what was going to happen as more people who joined us; what it would mean for my relationship with Rogue. But, we had to do this together.

We shot off the ocean floor and swam as fast as we could, ploughing our way through the water. The pressure got lighter and lighter and it began to seem easier to swim upwards as the light got brighter. It was then that we hit a dense patch of water, where once again we were suspended in eternity... before we found ourselves spluttering on the tiles in the fifth floor bathroom.

Epilogue

§§

"Where am I?"

"*Who are you? What are you doing here?*"

"Who are *you?* Where have you taken me?"

"I was not the one who brought you here. It is *you* who has invaded."

"I am not here by choice! I was forced! Where are you?"

The Destroyer was in a dark abyss. It couldn't see anything no matter how hard it looked. It was as though it had gone blind. The light airy voice that taunted it was nowhere to be seen. "What are you?" the voice asked.

"Destruction… Death… Chaos… I am Havoc."

"*Are you now…?*"

"What has happened to me? Where am I?"

A figure came out of the darkness, with long white hair and a blank, disinterested look on her face. "Here is where we dream. The Guardians have captured you… as they did me."

"Who are you?"

"I am Ariannah…" she answered. "I am the Deceiver."

195

www.ingramcontent.com/pod-product-compliance
Lightning Source LLC
Chambersburg PA
CBHW070028120726
47909CB00003B/1088